HAWKEYE
DENVER

DETERMINATION

HAWKEYE PROTECTORS: DENVER

SIERRA
CARTWRIGHT

USA TODAY BESTSELLING AUTHOR

DETERMINATION

First E-book Publication: March 2023

Line Editing by GG Royale

Proofing by Bev Albin, Cassie Hess-Dean, Whitney Cartwright De Luna

Layout Design by Once Upon An Alpha

Cover Design by Once Upon An Alpha

Photo provided by Depositphotos.com

Promotion by Once Upon An Alpha, Shannon Hunt

DEDICATION

For Shayla—couldn't have figured this one out on my own. And the sprint group. Your motivation and laughter keep me out of those pesky rabbit holes!
Bev, always.
I appreciate you all.

CHAPTER ONE

HAWKEYE

The moment Kane Patterson jogged up the last stair leading to the porch of the impressive mountain home, the door swung open to reveal a very beautiful Noelle Montrose, wife of one of his friends and coworkers at Hawkeye Security.

"Kane! I'm so glad you could make it." Her smile was wide and inviting.

He kissed her cheek "It's been a while."

"Since the wedding."

Had it been that long? "Two years?" How well he remembered the festive occasion. Yeah, he'd been genuinely happy to see Joe marry such a wonderful woman, but the occasion had been memorable for another reason, namely a gorgeous brunette he'd cradled against him for a sensual dance beneath the stars.

The lady in question, Morgan—a name he'd never forget —had made it clear she'd be open for so much more.

Fortunately his sanity returned before he did more than kiss her. And maybe break her heart. After all, he had a shitty track record with relationships.

"The guys are in Joe's office. Oh wait, you haven't been here before. Let me show you the way."

He followed her into the oversize home with its massive open spaces and soaring windows. "It's beautiful, Noelle."

"Thanks." Glancing over her shoulder, she responded, "We get up here as often as we can."

"But not as often as you'd like to."

"Exactly." She led the way down the hall to the last door on the left. "Go ahead and let yourself in. Hawkeye will be here in just a minute."

Interesting. "Hawkeye?" To what did they owe the honor of having the firm's owner show up? And a bigger question was why the hell had Kane been invited?

He'd returned to Denver last night after a too-damn-long stint in Africa. The mission had been fucked from the beginning. How was it possible to protect a businessman who knew he was at risk and not only ignored it, but taunted would-be kidnappers? He hadn't ended up dead, but that wasn't true for some local security guards.

Kane had earned some damn R&R and intended to take it.

Curious, he knocked sharply on the door before entering the decidedly masculine space. Though Joe had a large desk toward the back of the room, he also had a smaller table with comfortable leather chairs arranged around it.

Water was available, along with a pricey bottle of Bonds whiskey.

The two men in the room—Joe and Logan Powell, both Hawkeye team leaders—stood.

He shook Logan's hand. "You recovered?"

Logan responded in a fake British accent. "'Tis only a flesh wound." After the guys all grinned, he dropped the smile and teasing note. "Cell phone and tactical vest took the worst of it."

Still, catching a bullet hurt like a mofo. And Logan had gotten off easy. "Heard a rumor you're getting married."

"Got my head on right finally."

Maybe getting shot at had something to do with that.

After greetings were exchanged, Joe swept his hand wide to indicate everyone should take their seats. "Help yourself." He nodded toward the fine distillate.

Months had passed since Kane had been with his friends, and a drink appealed. If he had a glass, however, he might sleep for a week like his body demanded, and he needed to be conscious enough to make the drive back to his home in the Denver suburbs.

Though Kane had received and declined numerous invitations to the Montroses' well-regarded BDSM play parties, he'd never received a personal call from Joe requesting his presence thirty minutes before any of the other guests were scheduled to arrive.

As he took his seat, he scrubbed his hand down his face. *Shit.* He'd forgotten to shave. How many days in a row did that make it?

"How was Africa?" Logan asked.

What passed for small talk in this group. Combat. Death. Destruction.

Since all of them were former military and still dealt with secrets at the highest level, they tended—maybe unnecessarily—to keep their terminology somewhat vague. Didn't matter. They all understood the same language.

"The asset is back in the States." Meaning casualties had been sustained, but the company that had written the check to keep its arrogant CEO safe was happy.

Moments later Hawkeye entered the room, dressed for work in jeans, boots, a leather bomber jacket, and a ballcap pulled low over his eyebrows.

"Evening." Without waiting for anyone to shake his hand,

he took a seat. "I hate to mix business with pleasure."

Bullshit. If he was sincere, he wouldn't be doing it. This was one in a long series of calculated moves.

"All of you are aware we've been working an art case for months."

"Too fucking long," Logan chimed in.

Kane vaguely knew about it. Early on, Logan had called for a consult. Kane hadn't been helpful, but he'd provided a sounding board that his colleague appreciated.

Still, a question remained. *Why am I here?* Unless Hawkeye wanted to assign him to the task force.

"We've hit a lot of dead ends." Logan uncapped a bottle of water. "And there haven't been any more heists in weeks. Insurance company we're working for would fire us because of our admittedly frustrating lack of progress, but they've sustained so many losses that they don't have the resources they need to conduct all their own investigations. That doesn't mean they're not considering replacing us."

"We may have caught a break." Hawkeye leaned forward.

All eyes were on the boss.

"Last night, one of our operatives was in New Orleans for a bachelorette party, shopping at an antique store. Saw a small statue she thought she recognized, so she called her team leader."

Hawkeye Security sent out daily bulletins on high-profile cases. On every part of the globe, employees had received emails with pictures of missing pieces, just in case something like this happened. "Give that woman a raise."

"Already done." Without missing a beat, Hawkeye went on. "She pretended a casual interest in the piece and was told by the store manager it was there on consignment from an estate sale company."

Was it? Kane steepled his fingers. "Guessing that means no paperwork proving provenance."

"But no forged documents," Joe added.

"After everything is sorted out, the sculpture will be returned to its rightful owner. Who didn't sound happy about the news."

Very interesting.

Hawkeye allowed the information to sink in before going on. "This could mean nothing, but the store is owned by Holden's father."

The three other men exchanged glances.

"Pierce Holden?" Logan echoed. The two men were best friends, and Logan had just recruited him to join Hawkeye.

And he was the older brother of the sexy woman Kane had kissed at Joe and Noelle's wedding, Morgan Holden—the woman who fueled his nighttime fantasies.

"*Fuck.*" Logan poured a shot of whiskey. "Does Holden know?"

"No. He's out of town, at our Aiken Training Center in Nevada, remote maneuvers. You know the drill. No cell phone or technology." Hawkeye shrugged. "But I'm leaving the notification decision to you as team leader."

So the information was on a need-to-know basis.

Kane didn't envy Logan's position.

Without it being asked, Hawkeye addressed the question that had to loom large in everyone's minds. "As far as we know, he has zero interests in his family business."

Logan took a drink. "I believe that. Relationship between father and son is awkward, at best."

Hawkeye nodded. "And right now you could say he's under our surveillance."

Pretty damn shitty.

"Before he signed on with us, I told him about the Dallas store being hit."

"They weren't the only gallery," Hawkeye added. "Dozens, all over the country."

"Yeah. I asked him to see if he could gather any intel from his father. So far he's found out nothing."

Now another question loomed in Kane's mind. Was it possible Holden knew something he hadn't shared with Logan?

Hawkeye continued. "Preliminary research in the last few hours indicates that Gerard has a holding company of sorts. Since they're a private corporation, information isn't as available as it might be otherwise."

Not that Hawkeye let little details like that stop them.

"Here's what we have been able to ascertain—"

So far. No doubt the tech team had been digging in government files from all fifty states and had maybe started looking offshore.

"Holden Enterprises seem to own numerous businesses. Art galleries, of course, but also antique shops and a chain of women's clothing boutiques." He paused. "And an auction house."

Well, hell.

Logan whistled.

"Again, none of this indicates anything."

Of course not. But the auction house was a hell of a convenient set-up. The infrastructure was already in place to fence pieces. No wonder Hawkeye had called an after-hours meeting. "But this is the first piece that's been recovered?"

"To our knowledge," Logan confirmed. "Other insurance agencies and investigators, even feebs, may have intel we don't."

But Hawkeye Security now had a strand in the web that was being weaved around the bad guys. Someone, somewhere, knew something. There were connections, and Kane would look for them.

Logan nodded. "I'll get out there with a team."

"Let Inamorata know when you need the plane to be

ready." Hawkeye referenced his right-hand woman who was the organization's glue. Then Hawkeye leveled a glance at Kane. "You're due some R&R."

Duty calls. "That you're going to let me take in my next life?"

"It'll continue to accrue." As Hawkeye stood, he adjusted his ballcap. "You're reporting to Powell and heading logistics from here until he's back in town."

"Suits me. No one sees the big picture better than Patterson." Logan put down his now-empty glass. "We'll want to canvass all of the Holden galleries and shops."

"And look into their auction business," Kane guessed.

"Get with Inamorata on that as well. You'll have all the resources you need." With that, he studied his team leaders. "Let's get to work, gentlemen."

So fucking much for a relaxing weekend.

After gulping a deep steadying breath, Morgan pulled open the front door to the Reserve, downtown Denver's premier BDSM club. She'd entered the same way a dozen times before but for vanilla purposes. The owners hosted meetups to introduce newbies to the surroundings, the rules, and BDSM in general. Attendance was mandatory in order to become a member.

Though she had experimented with some of the club's Dominants to get a sense of what types of play she preferred, she'd never actually participated in a scene. This evening, her nerves seemed to be wrapped in barbed wire.

The moment Morgan stepped into the well-lit foyer, Harmony, the receptionist, looked up with a reassuring smile. "I saw your name on the list, but I wasn't sure if you'd show up."

She was as surprised as Harmony seemed to be. On at least three occasions, Morgan had made a reservation but chickened out at the last minute.

"The last time we talked, you weren't sure whether you wanted to use a scene name or not."

She'd been pondering that. "How about MJ?" Since the abbreviation was a stand-in for Morgan Jayne, her first and middle names, at least it might not be too difficult to remember.

Harmony slid some paperwork across the podium toward Morgan. "I just need your signature on these pages."

She scanned the information. A copy of the rules that she'd already received, procedures of what to do if anything made her uncomfortable.

After exhaling, she set down the pen and gave the file folder back to Harmony.

"You remember the club safe word?"

This was gone over repeatedly. "Skiing."

"Relax and have fun. That's the most important thing. You're here to enjoy yourself."

"Enjoy." She nodded as her heart raced. "This is me having fun." Her fake smile made Harmony laugh.

"For your first few times, we'll keep an extra eye out for you. Tristan is on duty."

The club's head dungeon monitor.

"And Master Soren will be in attendance."

One of the three owners.

"Feel free to ask them questions."

Morgan nodded.

"The bar is open, but only sodas, energy drinks, or mock-tails if you're scening."

"Got it."

Harmony smiled again. "This makes you an official member now. Welcome to the Reserve, MJ."

During the short time that she chatted with Harmony and handled mundane details, Morgan had started to relax. That lasted until she entered the dungeon with its thumping primal music and dim lights.

Every time she'd been here, music had been low or nonexistent. At most there'd been two dozen people. This evening there were at least fifty attendees, perhaps more.

Needing a moment to center herself, she avoided the public places where people were playing and instead walked to the locker room.

At first, she'd found the mandatory premembership meetings onerous. But now she was grateful she knew the employees, a few members, and her way around. It gave her a sense of comfort that would be missing otherwise.

She found a locker, then removed her coat and exchanged her flats for sexy heels that she ordinarily lacked the courage to wear.

Before exiting, she glanced in the mirror to be sure that her short, form-hugging black dress covered her butt cheeks. She'd never dressed like this before.

Her selection had been intentional. If she scened, she could just lift it up, which meant she would retain a modicum of modesty. No way was she ready for a bare midriff or more risqué BDSM or fetish wear.

As a group of women entered laughing and giggling, she squared her shoulders and made her way toward the bar.

After receiving a cranberry juice with a splash of lemon-lime soda, she swiveled her stool. From where she was, she had a view of most of the entire space. What was better than people watching?

She scanned the surroundings to be sure she didn't see anyone she knew from her personal life. Though the possibility was remote, it still existed.

Each week, she attended happy hour with a close group

of friends, nicknamed the Carpe Diem Divas. Most of them were into BDSM. But Noelle—one of the Divas—along with her husband, Joe, hosted play parties at their home in the foothills.

As far as Morgan knew, none of them were members of the Reserve, but unlikely didn't mean impossible.

Finally, as though it was a shot of courage, she drained the last of her beverage.

"Another?" the bartender offered.

"Maybe later."

"No one here is going to bite you." Mandy, the bartender, took away the empty glass. With a grin, she added, "Unless you ask nicely."

Laughing, more relaxed, she slid off the barstool.

Now what?

Classes had included discussions of protocol, relationship dynamics, reminders that there was not one true way of practicing BDSM, the difference between a Top and bottom, Dominant and sub, even Master and slave dynamics. There were demonstrations and practice time, but none of the comprehensive instructions included advice on how to go up to a complete stranger and ask him if he wanted to spank her ass.

A little bit at a loss, she crossed to a cupping demonstration and stood next to a bunch of people who seemed to be paired up.

Morgan exhaled. She'd underestimated how much more difficult it was to be here all alone, feeling awkward, than she imagined—and she'd imagined it being terrible. No wonder a lot of people came on the buddy system. At least it would be easier once she'd made friends.

"Hey. Glad to see you."

She turned. *Frank.* He was a Top she remembered from one of her meetings.

With a smile, as if they'd never met, he extended his hand. "Lars. Sir Lars."

Pretentious much?

Still, she took his hand, and his grip was more forceful than she'd anticipated, as if he had something to prove. With a mental sigh, she responded, remembering to use her made-up name. "MJ."

He nodded. "My pleasure, MJ."

The conversation ended there.

After she pulled away from him, they stood there staring at each other. Seconds later, to cover the awkward silence, she tried again. "Have you been coming often?"

"Every weekend."

"So this isn't unfamiliar anymore." She wished she could fast forward time so that it was the same for her.

He cocked his head to the side at her. "Looking for anything in particular?"

Right now she was close to getting what she'd come here for. But she hesitated. Why, she wasn't sure. "Observing for now."

"You've disappointed me."

The words rang with a note of condemnation. The old Morgan would have apologized and likely acquiesced to assuage his ego. But rejection after rejection, being told she was too emotional, had toughened her, and she tilted her chin, refusing to back down.

"I'd like you to reconsider."

"She won't."

That voice… That tone… Morgan would know it anywhere, and her knees wobbled.

Kane Patterson. The last man she ever wanted to see again. The same one she'd thrown herself at in a regrettable moment of utter weakness. The same one who'd kissed her before brutally sending her away.

11

To make it worse, he was going to be her brother's teammate, and he was close with men three of the Divas were involved with.

This moment had to be one of the worst of her life.

Trying to keep herself focused, she dug her fingers into her palms as she turned to face him. Now, as then, he took her breath away.

He was well over six feet tall, with dark hair, almost obsidian eyes, a formidable, square jaw, and a long, faint scar on one cheek that somehow made him all the more handsome.

In a tux at Noelle and Joe's wedding on that fateful night, he'd been gorgeous. Now, in form-fitting jeans that highlighted his tight rear, seen-better-days boots, and a black T-shirt that showed off his ridiculously large biceps, he was mouthwatering.

Damn it. This couldn't be happening.

"Who the hell are you?" Lars demanded.

"Kane Patterson, former military. And the lady's protector."

Jackass. Had he always been this way?

"The fuck?" Lars demanded.

Equally as confused, she blinked.

Puffing up, Lars went on. "That's not for you to say."

"It is now."

"Kane…" What the hell was going on here? She grabbed hold of his forearm, then wished she hadn't as awareness of his strength arced through her.

If he registered her grip, he didn't acknowledge it.

"The lady is with me. Any questions?"

Lars looked at her. "As far as I know, the lady can speak for herself."

"Now you know differently," Kane warned.

Flashing fire, Morgan swung toward Kane. "How dare

12

you?" He'd painfully rejected her, and now he was behaving like a Neanderthal?

At that moment, Soren joined them and smiled at her. "MJ."

The owner was wearing leather pants and a dark button-up shirt open almost to his waist. Damn. She'd had no idea he was so lean with six-pack abs.

"Gentlemen." He nodded at the two Dominants currently engaged in a pissing contest.

Then she amended her thought. One was no doubt a Dominant. The other was someone hopelessly out of his depth.

"Problem, MJ?" Soren asked.

"MJ?" Kane repeated.

Soren leveled a glance at him that would shut up an ordinary man. "One more word and I'll bounce your ass out of here."

Kane folded his arms though his dark expression shouted that he would tear the man from limb to limb if he attempted it.

"MJ?" Soren prompted.

"This man"—Lars darted an incredulous finger toward Kane.—"says MJ is under his protection. And that's BS."

Soren held up a hand. "Both of you will *shut the fuck up.* Am I understood?"

Though they continued to glower at each other, they remained silent.

"MJ, if you will?" Soren stepped aside and beckoned her to join him.

She was hyperaware of other attendees shooting interested glances in their direction. Morgan wasn't sure she'd ever been more embarrassed.

Without touching her he indicated a small alcove near a picture of the Maroon Bells, one of Colorado's most photographed sites. At least here, they'd have a small amount of privacy.

"You've had an interesting first thirty minutes."

"I'm so sorry, Sir. I never wanted to have the club owner intervene on my behalf, let alone on my first night. This kind of stuff never happens to me. Really, I'm the world's most boring person."

"Clearly not." His grin—and the reassuring look in his eyes—took the sting from his words.

She shot a glance at the other two men who were still facing one another, inches apart.

"Unless my guess is wrong, you have some sort of past with Master Kane."

And she'd come here for privacy. "If you can call it that."

"He seems to think he has a right to make a claim on you."

He'd abdicated that right when he sent her away with tears burning her eyes.

"At the Reserve, you get to dictate the rules of engagement, no matter what happens outside it. If you want both of those idiots tossed out on their asses with a temporary ban, I'll make it happen."

She shook her head. "That won't be necessary."

"I'm assuming you're not under Master Kane's protection?"

"No, Sir."

"Would you like to be?"

"Honestly I don't even know what that means."

"If you opt to continue a discussion with him this evening, you'll want to talk about that with him. Essentially when a newer bottom enters the scene, they may opt to have a Top look out for them. If you accepted his protection, all contacts and requests to scene with you would go through him. He'd vet the person before passing along any information to you. Some bottoms will wear a collar—often something very informal on their wrist or ankle to signify the bond. At times such formality exists. And of course, there are as many ways..."

She smiled. He didn't need to finish his sentence since she'd heard it so many times in class. "To practice BDSM as there are participants."

"You *were* paying attention."

Maybe he wouldn't think as badly of her now.

"Of course, you're more than welcome to tell him to fuck off."

Sounded appealing, and she knew it was what she should do. But unfortunately, remnants of the old Morgan—the one who'd had a panty melting reaction to the way he'd held her —was still there, even if she hadn't been seen for a while.

"What will it be?"

Even if she took Soren up on his offer to kick both of them out and leave her alone for the rest of the evening, she'd only earn a reprieve.

Soren enforced his rules inside these walls, but outside them, Kane was a force of nature, a special operator accustomed to kicking in doors and never giving up until he accomplished his mission. Even if every odd was against him.

Sooner or later, she'd have to face him. "I'll deal with this, Sir."

"Very good." Approval radiated from Soren's gaze.

During the time she'd been coming here, she'd learned BDSM was about a power exchange. Submissives and bottoms had power along with a responsibility to determine his or her own limits.

"Before I allow you to return, you're familiar with the club safe word."

She hated being in a position where he felt it necessary to ask. "Skiing, Sir."

Though he stepped aside, he remained nearby: observing, listening, making her wonder about his background as well.

"Thank you for your offer, Lars." For a moment she was tempted to add, "Perhaps another time." But she kept her mouth shut. The truth was, she wasn't attracted to him. Though that shouldn't be a requirement for a scene, she was sure. But it mattered to her. "But I'm going to pass for tonight and in the future."

Kane waved his fingers as if brushing an insect from his arm. "Move along."

After snarling at Kane and Soren, then glowering at her, he headed for the exit.

She took a breath and addressed Kane. "As for you..." He crackled with the force of an electrical field. Even though she shouldn't be, she was drawn to the frustrating alpha male. "We need to have a discussion about what being under your protection means."

His grin was laced with triumph, and he possessively cupped her shoulders, melting her.

He glanced at Soren. "The lady has spoken. Now fuck off."

Hastily she pointed out the obvious to Kane. "I didn't agree to anything."

In a way so that no one else could overhear, he leaned toward her. "Oh but you will, sweetheart. You will."

Keeping her distance might be a battle she couldn't win. "I only said I would discuss it."

"Mmm-hmm." Though he appeared to be playing by the rules, he was obliterating them all. "Does the bar suit you? Or perhaps you'd prefer one of the upstairs rooms."

Where they'd have much more privacy.

"The bar." Soren took the answer from her. "I'm not open to compromise."

Kane nodded tightly. "The bar it is."

CHAPTER TWO

HAWKEYE

As if they were a couple, Kane took her hand and guided her to the back of the club.

There were empty seats at the far side of the bar next to a woman with an untouched bottle of water in front of her. She wore a pantsuit with a button-up blouse. A Domme? Or a guest wearing street clothes?

The moment he seemed to notice the same woman that Morgan did, Kane changed their path, leading them in the opposite direction.

To be as far away as possible? "Problem?"

"Cop."

Morgan shook her head. "Do you know her?"

"I recognize the look."

"The look?" What does that even mean? "Are you sure?"

He glanced at her and raised one eyebrow, and she sighed. No doubt he'd had enough training and maybe worked with federal agents in the past. "Is there anything for us to worry about?"

"No." He paused. "The club operates within the confines of the law."

Did that mean certain other things, other people even, did not?

"You can ask more questions later. This is neither the time nor the place."

Once again she was reminded they moved in different worlds. He was much like her brother, always responding to questions in a way that was somewhere between vague and obscure.

Mandy appeared a few moments later and placed napkins in front of them.

"The same as earlier," Morgan ordered. "Cranberry juice with a splash of lemon-lime soda."

Then Kane placed his order. "Whatever energy drink you have."

"You got it."

"Not planning to sleep anytime soon?" she asked him.

He shook his head. "When I get some R&R maybe."

She'd seen her brother, Pierce, push that hard as well. "Working all the time can't be good for you."

"It's the only life I know."

Another warning she'd be wise to heed. Instead, she was sitting here next to him, stupidly close. And he took hold of her stool and swiveled the top so that she faced him. He filled her vision, swamped her senses. With the way he'd positioned himself, it was as if they were by themselves in this crowded, noisy space.

Once their drinks were in front of them, she asked the question that kept running through her mind. "What the hell is wrong with you?"

Annoyingly he responded with a question of his own. "Want to explain why you're here?"

"No." She swept her hair back from her forehead. "It's none of your business." *None of anyone's.*

"Joe and Noelle have play parties."

Was he always this persistent? "I know."

"It's safer there. People you know who'll watch out for you."

Despite her resolve, she responded to his observation. "And my brother may show up."

"Ah." He nodded. "Worried about him being overprotective?"

"Among other things." Having him look at her bare butt. Maybe seeing more of him than she ever wanted.

And then there was one of her best friends, Ella. They'd been close since high school, and Pierce had rescued them one night after someone spiked the punch at a party. Without her knowing it, he'd saved Ella again recently at a honky-tonk when she was being harassed by an entitled asshole lawyer. The two had hit it off and were now planning to get married. She couldn't be happier for them. But that didn't mean she wanted to see her friend get spanked by her big brother.

"So what are you looking for? Need your ass paddled, sweetheart?"

She turned slightly to pick up her drink and stir her straw into it. "Not by you."

As if her words stung him, he winced.

"Look, Kane, I have no idea what the hell all that was about with…" She paused, searching for Frank's scene name. "Lars." The two had puffed up like peacocks putting on a ridiculous show that others had seemed to enjoy. "I don't know what you were thinking. But I neither want nor need your protection."

"Well, you've got it."

"As you so succinctly told Soren, *'Fuck off.'*" Her protest was forced, more conjured than real. The truth was every part of her responded to his rugged masculinity.

Still, he'd rejected her previously, and she'd rushed from

the dance floor drowning in abject humiliation. She'd opened herself to him once and been vulnerable. No way would she go through that again.

"It's not that easy."

She sighed. "It is. You go do whatever you came here for and leave me to play with whoever I want to."

"I didn't like the way he was looking at you."

"What?" She scowled at him. Lars's conversation had been normal. At least until Kane showed up. "I have no idea what you mean."

"He wanted to devour you."

"Which you don't."

"You're wrong about that, sweetheart."

Mouth agape, she had no response.

Pressing his advantage, he leaned toward her. "I'll ask again. Why are you here?"

"You're the secret agent man. You tell me."

"I already did. You want your sweet little ass spanked. And I'm happy to indulge you."

Anyone but you. So why was he the only one she wanted?

"You have to admit you're curious."

"No." *No, no, no.* As she momentarily glanced away, she shook her head.

"Little liar. He laughed, low and seductive, bringing her back to face him, not letting her hide. "You *are* curious. Two years have changed nothing between us."

"They've changed everything." She placed her drink back on the bar, so the contents didn't splash over the rim. "I'm no longer the same woman."

"No? So why are you breathing fast? Why are your lips parted? Why are you looking at me with wide, beautiful golden eyes?"

He was right, and she hated that he saw her so completely. "Kane…"

"What could the harm be?"

"Harm?" She'd had plenty of experience with that. He was a man who could break her heart if given half a chance, and they both knew it.

"You can trust me to be a gentleman."

"Is that what you call it?"

"Look…MJ…" He dug his hands into his hair, for the first time seemingly at a bit of a loss of what to say or maybe how to phrase it. "At the wedding… If we hadn't ended—"

"You." She brought up her chin. "You ended it."

"Fine. If I hadn't had the sense to stop when I did, I'd have thrown you beneath me in a hotel room and fucked you senseless."

"And then what?" In that moment, that had been what she wanted, craved.

"I had to report for duty. How would you have felt after giving me every part of yourself, body and soul?" He waited, then repeated himself. "I would have left you in that bed, alone. Would that have been better?"

"You're trying to make me believe you were doing me a kindness."

"Oh, sweetheart. Yeah." When he went on, his voice was low and gruff. "You have no idea what it cost me."

He left her breathless.

"But one thing life taught me? I'm honest with myself. I know who I am. I'm shit at relationships, as my ex-wife can tell you."

She had no idea he'd been married; he didn't seem like the type.

"I'm never home. Too wrapped up in my job and in myself." He placed his hands on either side of her hips. "I meant it when I told you it was for your own good."

Morgan squared her shoulders. "You know what? I am damn tired of men telling me how to think and how to act.

And that goes for your ridiculous assertion of protection. I can *and will* make my own decisions."

He inclined his head.

"I know what I want, and I'm capable of getting it," she went on.

"So what is that, exactly? A no-strings attached BDSM scene?"

She remained quiet and forced herself to stay still so she didn't nod and give herself away.

"I can give you that."

At what cost?

"As I've said, you know you can trust me. I'll give you a safe, memorable first experience."

She blinked. "You're assuming a lot." He couldn't know she'd never done this before.

"Am I?" Rather than waiting for a response, he went on. "Sweetheart, you're new to the scene. You have a basic comfort and familiarity with the club, which tells me you've gone through the orientation process. But you didn't have a clue how to interact and get what you need. I overheard you with Lars."

How long had he been eavesdropping?

"You didn't come out and ask for what you wanted. Instead, you engaged in small talk."

He saw all that? And more, no doubt.

"You went to classes. Probably even took notes."

She had.

"Maybe you saw some demos, perhaps participated in a few."

Since he knew everything, she didn't need to answer.

"What interested you?"

Slowly but surely he was reeling her in. What would those big, strong hands feel like on her body?

"Flogging? Saint Andrew's cross? Spanking bench. A little

suspension?" As he spoke, he dropped his voice even lower, forcing her to lean forward to hear him.

With his voice, he was weaving an intimate, compelling web she didn't want to escape. He was turning her on as he exploited all her desires. This wasn't about impact play; it was about emotional connection. It was as satisfying as it was dangerous.

"An over-the-knee spanking?"

In her lap, she twisted her hands together.

"That's it, isn't it?" He smiled, slow and conqueringly.

He really was watching her, paying attention to every response.

"That's what you want."

"Uh…" *No. Yes.*

Kane released his grip on her, then stood to offer his hand. "The choice is yours. I can meet your greatest fantasies, or I can do as you say and fuck off."

As if paralyzed, she remained where she was.

"I see." He nodded tightly. "In that case, have a good evening, MJ. I hope you find what you're looking for." Then he saluted her, turned away, and walked off.

What was she thinking? She wanted it, even if she was taking the first step toward her own heartbreak. "Kane!"

He stopped and slowly pivoted.

"Wait." She closed her eyes for a moment before she took a breath and shakily climbed down from the barstool.

In an instant, Kane closed the distance between them. She didn't have to go to him or meet him halfway; he came to her.

With tenderness, he captured her face between his strong palms. "Thank you for your trust."

Closing her eyes for a brief second, she prayed it wasn't misplaced. "We have an agreement, right? Just one scene."

He hesitated for a moment before answering. "Tonight?"

"I mean, you're going to deploy again. Or whatever you call it, right?"

"The word works."

"You can leave at a moment's notice."

"Right now, I'm on a Denver-based assignment."

"For how long?" she pressed.

"Until I receive new orders."

That's the way it seemed to work for Pierce as well, which was one of the problems Ella had dealt with.

But the news reassured her, and she nodded. Scening with him this evening was fine because it was risk-free. No complications. Before she knew it, he'd be gone, and she wouldn't have to worry about running into him.

"Back to your question... If I meet your needs and you want to see me again, we can make it happen."

Two years ago, those were the words she dreamed of hearing. And now they scared her. Once would be enough. She needed to protect herself.

Deep down, a tiny voice whispered that it might already be too late. She shook her head to clear it. "And since we didn't finish the earlier conversation, I am not under your protection."

He growled.

The sound was as primitive as it was menacing.

"As I told you, I know who I am. If I'm here when you are and I see you getting ready to make a mistake, I can't promise that I will keep my mouth shut. In fact, I can promise that I won't stand by and watch."

"I'm not your concern."

"Here, away from the safety of all of your friends and your safety net, you *are* my concern."

Frustrated, she exhaled. Kane Patterson was a total alpha —annoyingly so— all the way through.

"But since I don't want to be unreasonable, I won't make you wear a collar…"

A collar? Her breath caught.

With an agonizingly gentle touch, he traced the pad of his thumb down the column of her throat.

"To publicly claim you as mine. Though you would look beautiful in one."

At the wedding, her feminine intuition had recognized his powerful aura. But she'd had no idea the level of danger he represented.

"Take me as I am, sweetheart." He tipped his head to the side. "If we go forward, I cannot—will not—walk away from my responsibility to you." Before she could respond, he went on. "No matter how hard you protest."

"Has anyone mentioned how annoying you are?"

"Women, you mean?" When she nodded, he went on. "On multiple occasions."

At least she was in good company.

"I have my toy bag in a locker, if we are in agreement."

Agreement? He had an interesting way of seeing the world. What he meant was she had to go along with his dictate if she wanted to play.

"But I'm thinking my hand might suit you better." He stroked his thumb lower, then placed two fingers at the hollow of her throat. "What do you say? Would you like the spanking you've fantasized about?"

She frowned at his assumption.

"Of course you've been fantasizing. You wouldn't be here otherwise."

No other man had had the ability to read her mind like this.

Gulping, she nodded.

"I promise you won't regret it, sweetheart." He leaned forward to drop the gentlest of kisses on her forehead.

His tenderness was her kryptonite.

Once again, he took her hand and led her back into the dungeon.

"You were watching the cupping earlier."

"Mostly because I was trying to get comfortable being here, and I didn't know what else to do."

"Any interest in trying it or watching again?"

"Not at this time." Though she'd never really considered it, once she had more courage, she might be willing to try.

Still holding onto her, keeping her close, he guided her toward the section of the area that contained numerous Saint Andrew's crosses.

At one station a bottom was being flogged.

Morgan missed a step. The expression on the woman's face was sublime, as if she were in a state of bliss, unaware of anything except what was happening to her. Even though the club's loud music drowned the Top's words, Morgan could tell he continuously spoke to the bottom he was flogging.

Kane draped his arm around her shoulder in a way that was far too possessive to be comforting.

How long she stood there, she had no idea, but Kane did not attempt to hurry her along, seemingly content to watch along with her until the woman was being released from her bonds. "I've heard of people getting lost in a scene, but that's the first time I've watched it happen."

"A beautiful sight, isn't it?"

"Transcendent."

Though he studied her intently, he didn't respond to her comment.

A full thirty seconds later, he spoke again. "Not all scenes are like that. Getting into subspace is a fabulous experience when it happens, but I can't recommend that it be a goal in and of itself. The couple may have been together for a very long time, or she has given her Top explicit direction about

26

what she wants. There's no doubt they are both experienced players."

"Are you warning me in advance not to expect something like that from you, Sir?" God help her. Where had that come from? Not just the teasing but the honorific. He wasn't her Dominant, and she didn't have to call him that.

"Sweetheart…" He turned toward her to capture her chin. "I'll give you anything you desire. You just have to buy the ticket and take the ride."

She doubted something like that was possible for her. She would have to be willing to let go emotionally. And that was something she wasn't ready to do.

As they moved on, they passed a few couches. From her classes she knew they weren't just for conversations; they were a place where Tops could provide aftercare to their bottoms at the end of a scene.

For a few minutes they watched a rigging demonstration with intricate, stunning rope work. While cameras generally weren't permitted at the club, a sign said a professional was on site to video this particular scene. Only the participants were in the camera's lens, and the backdrop was a large green canvas, meaning the location could be anywhere.

"Thoughts on this?"

"It looks uncomfortable, and my body definitely does not contort into those kinds of angles." With one leg behind her, up near her rear, the woman's position was mind-boggling. At Morgan's occasional yoga class, staying in place for downward dog could be a challenge, and despite practice at home, she still couldn't do a backbend. "But I appreciate the artistry."

"Rope bondage doesn't have to include suspension or those kinds of positions."

"Maybe…" Not that it would happen with him.

They wandered around some more, and again he seemed infinitely patient.

He was giving her the kind of outing she'd been hoping for—someone to share experience with plenty of discussion time. As they walked and talked, she was getting a better idea of what intrigued her.

In another area, almost all of the spanking benches were occupied as were a couple of the suspension rings. In a quiet corner, a bottom was laying on her back with her Top relentlessly bringing her to orgasm with a massive vibrator.

She squirmed, and Kane shot a glance in her direction. "I'd say that goes on your 'maybe' list."

"No."

"No?"

"It's on my 'oh fuck yes' list."

He laughed. "Noted for future reference."

Even though their time was already ticking away.

"Have you seen enough?"

She nodded, and he led her toward the main entrance where there was a lounge area with lots of couches and chairs, even a couple of twin beds.

"Do you prefer somewhere more private? Or perhaps in the middle of the action?"

Since they'd already been the center of attention in a negative way, she opted for something a little more secluded. "How about that one?" She pointed to a chaise longue.

"That will work."

He sat, and she remained standing, hands folded in front of her.

"In addition to the club's safe word, you have one of your own?"

She nodded. "I'm going to stick with red." At least it was easy to remember. One woman in orientation had selected watermelon. Morgan wasn't sure she'd be able to get that out if she were in pain or fear.

"And for slow? Yellow?"

"Yes."

"Excellent."

Now that the moment was here, she was petrified, and like he'd already ascertained, she was a newbie with no clue what to do. Stay where she was? Drop to her knees? Lower herself over his lap?

With a passion, she hated being stuck in this moment, swimming in a morass of doubts and fears.

"You're doing fine." Shocking her, he gently took her hand. "Come sit next to me."

Confused, she blinked. "What?"

His voice compassionate, he explained. "No way am I spanking your ass when you look like you're about to bolt for the door."

Was she that transparent? Or was he so tuned in to her?

He rubbed the inside of her wrist, making circles on her thready pulse.

"I'd say you're in the cardio zone."

"Is there something beyond that? Like anaerobic?" Didn't that mean she was barely able to breathe, or something like that?

"Come here, sweetheart."

Gulping she did, and he once more draped an arm around her shoulders and drew soothing circles on her upper arm. Unlike before, this time she drew comfort from it.

"At the bar, you had no hesitation about speaking your mind."

"This is different though."

"Is it?" He angled himself so he could look in her eyes. "How so?"

"We're entering a scene, right?"

"There's no need to second-guess yourself. I'll be clear with my expectations. Until then, keep being your spitfire self."

She exhaled. This should be easier than it was. "I have no idea how you want me to act. I don't even know what you want me to call you."

"You've already called me *Sir.*"

"That was an accident."

"Was it? Or perhaps it was an acknowledgement of the truth?"

His question was a challenge, and not wanting to lie, she blinked. "I mean, it was like…" *What?* Spontaneous, maybe?

"Natural?"

She hated that he was right.

"Inevitable, even."

Fight-or-flight instinct nipping at her, she gulped.

"Kane is fine for now." Then he went on. "To be clear, when we're in a scene, I'm happy if you get lost inside your head. I will watch out for you." He glanced around.

She followed the direction of his gaze.

"And so is Tristan."

The head dungeon monitor. He stood to one side, observing them.

"I take it you don't do well with supervision."

"Never needed it." He inclined his head. "And I like others to stay the fuck out of my business."

"Imagine that."

His words and their banter helped dissipate some of her budding tension.

"We have a couple of options here. I can swing my legs over the side as if I'm sitting in a chair. I can have you over my lap, and your fingers can touch the floor."

This sounded almost clinical when she expected him to

just pull her over his lap and wail on her poor backside. As usual, she might have underestimated him.

"Or I can remain where I am while you lie across my lap with your feet on the floor and your butt appealingly displayed for my chastisement."

Her pulse which had slowly been returning to normal suddenly accelerated again. Damn him. He used his words to heart-racing maximum effect. The image he'd painted was evocative, filling her mind.

"Another option which I call wheelbarrow involves you facing away from me kind of in a reverse cowgirl position."

With her pussy on his cock? She couldn't help but glance at him. A rock-hard erection pushed against his jeans.

Maybe he hadn't been lying when he said she'd have been beneath him that first night as he fucked her senseless.

In a way, the sight of his arousal relieved her. She didn't want to be the only one dealing with this kind of sexual demand.

"You'd be facedown on the leather." He continued to talk even though she was staring at his dick. "And because of the angle of the chaise, you'd be at a slight downward slope. I'll keep you in place, and you can hold the edges or the end for support. No matter which option you choose, I won't be able to see your expression which is somewhat unfortunate for me. Is it a problem for you?"

"Not at all." She could hide better that way.

"I will tune into your reactions to see where you are."

She nodded. "Uhm, do you have a preference of what we do?"

"Not at all. But thank you for asking. I anticipate that you may kick and thrash. If you're standing and draped across my lap, I can trap your legs between mine. If you're across me, you'll have less leverage. And if you're in the final position, your shoes could be a weapon if you're unable to stay still. So I'd have you remove them, which would be a pity because I like looking at your legs in them."

His compliments were addictive, making her mind flash an urgent warning not to take him too seriously.

"Decision made?"

"I think I'll go for the third option."

A smile sauntered across his lips, and his obsidian-colored eyes lightened a bit. "Excellent."

Is that what he'd been hoping for?

"Tell me what you're comfortable with as far as the state of your undress."

Club rules allowed for a lot, thongs and bare breasts as long as nipples were covered in the more public areas of the space.

She had mentally rehearsed this moment a thousand times. "I'll be keeping on my panties."

He nodded. "And your dress?"

"I'm comfortable with having it around my waist."

"So you're keeping your top half covered."

"Yes." She nodded primly.

"Understood. Anything I need to be aware of?"

"That covers it."

"I will keep my hands away from your pussy."

God save her. He'd broken the word out into two sexy syllables, rocketing sparks of awareness through her.

"It won't be easy." His voice was serious, as if he meant it.

"If you decide you want to be touched or brought to orgasm, you will have to ask for it."

That would not be happening.

"You're familiar with being warmed up?"

"I've heard of it, yes." Supposedly the act brought blood flow to the area and helped prevent bruising.

"A couple more questions before we get started."

"Sir?" She tipped her head to the side.

"Would you like to lift up your dress before we begin, or shall I do it for you?"

"Uhm…" The moment was suddenly very real. "You can."

"Would it be acceptable for me to gather your panties between your legs?"

Exposing her bare bottom to him.

"For your safety, I would like to be able to see any marks so I can adjust the intensity if needed."

His voice was so damn intimate, but his reasoning was sound.

A lot of the bottoms in the classes had worn thongs, so his request wasn't out of line. She folded her hands in front of her. "Well, if you need to, Sir." His earlier words returned. The night of the wedding, she was so vulnerable that she would have stripped down and welcomed him between her legs. Maybe he *had* saved her from herself.

He adjusted their positions and offered his hand. "Straddle me."

With those words, his tone was different, and the pitch was lower than before, containing a note of authority. His Dom voice? No matter what it was, a ribbon of response unfurled in her. In this moment, she had zero doubt he could get her to do anything he wanted.

Effortlessly he closed his hands around her waist and moved her into the position he wanted.

Then they were mere inches from each other. So close she inhaled his raw, spicy scent that was laced with primitive need. His dick pressed against her, making her grateful for the layers of clothing between them.

For a moment, she thought he might kiss her. If he did, heaven save her, she would let him.

He leaned forward slightly to remove her shoes and drop them onto the floor. "Good. Now use my shoulders to turn yourself around."

It took a lot of wiggling and some core strength for her to do that, making her clit grind against his jeans. But he didn't seem to object.

He parted his legs, and she maneuvered herself into the awkward position. What made her think she could do any type of wheelbarrow?

"You have a very delectable booty, MJ."

"Did you really call it that?" She laughed.

"Caboose?"

"Stop!" Was he trying to help dissipate her tension? Because the last thing she associated with him was a good sense of humor. Just the opposite. From what she'd seen, he was serious enough to freeze the fires of hell.

"Are you ready?"

She grabbed the sides of the chaise in a death grip. "I am." Then her instincts kicked in, and she surrendered to them. *"Sir."*

For a moment he didn't move, didn't say anything, drawing out her nervous anguish.

Slowly he began to caress the backs of her legs.

He was a study in contradictions. He told the club owner to fuck off, and now he was more tender than any other man had ever been with her.

This wasn't what she expected from a spanking warmup.

Without speaking, he continued for a few moments before moving to the insides of her thighs, taking care to avoid her needy apex.

Gradually he changed up what he was doing, making his strokes longer and firmer, turning her on. She was glad she'd put guardrails around their behavior so that she didn't throw herself at him again.

He lifted her dress to rub her buttocks, and unable to help herself, she moaned. She'd been prepared for an explosion of pain once he started, not this deliciously sensual slow burn.

"How's that?"

She turned her head slightly to the side so that he would be able to hear her answer. "I'm fine, Sir."

"Fine? Then I need to do better."

Please.

"If I ask again, please raise your thumb to indicate you are all right and that you're still on green."

Since the position would muffle her voice, she appreciated his extra safety measure.

"Because this is your first time, I'll give you no more than twenty strokes."

Would that be enough? Too much? Or not nearly enough?

"Are you ready?"

"Yes."

But he continued to rub. No doubt her butt cheeks were jiggling in a way she might ordinarily be self-conscious of, but right now she didn't care. She just wanted him to get on with it.

"I'm going to lift your dress."

"You're talking too much."

"Did you say something, sweetheart?"

"No!" Frantically she shook her head. "No, Sir." A whisper of cool air from the overhead fan brushed across her bare skin.

"Now your panties."

He captured the material and tucked it into place. "Your skin is a pretty pink color. So it will likely turn red. You may have tiny marks tomorrow, even my handprint."

She would like that.

Now that she was mostly naked in front of him, he vigorously rubbed her before giving her the first spank. Immediately afterward, he pressed his fingertips against the spot to take away the hurt.

"How was that?"

A little underwhelming. After all that teasing, she was ready for more and offered him two thumbs up.

He delivered three more in the same vicinity. And as always, he repeated the same process to take away the sting. When he reached five, he moved on to the other buttock and continued.

"You're halfway done."

She nodded.

"You're familiar with the sit spot?"

"Yes." The tender area between her upper thighs and the bottom of her ass. From what she'd heard, it was the ideal place for spanking.

When he continued, the swats were faster and harder, burning her skin, making her squirm, even gyrate her hips as arousal poured through her.

She had no idea where they were as far as the count was concerned and frankly didn't care as long as it went on and on.

He finished her off and rubbed her ass. "Gorgeous. Red is my new favorite color."

Every part of her body was inflamed. Though she hadn't been sure what to expect, she hadn't been prepared for the experience to be magical.

Suddenly he was helping her to sit up, pulling her underwear back into place, smoothing the material of her dress over her hips.

His arms wrapped around her, he held her on his lap.

His cock pressed insistently against her bottom. That she did that to him filled her with feminine power.

"Are you doing okay?"

"Yes," she murmured. She wanted to do it a hundred times over. Then she acknowledged the truth: even that might not be enough.

He held her for a very long time until she roused herself.

"How was that?" he asked.

"It wasn't bad." She shrugged. "I mean for a first experience."

He captured her chin, and though he smiled, his eyes were dark, foreboding. "You're treading a dangerous line, sweetheart."

"Am I?" Who knew she was so reckless?

Unable to help herself, she snuggled against his shoulder and yawned. She shouldn't be tired, but suddenly the only thing she wanted was to sleep.

And if she wasn't careful, she'd drift off in the sweet peace of his arms.

Since she couldn't allow that to happen, she pressed a hand to her chest. "Really? It was amazing."

He smiled. "I assume you have a purse or bag? Street clothes?"

"Shoes that I can actually walk in."

"If you're ready to leave, I'll walk you to your car."

"That's sweet, but I'm fine, really. The parking lot is well lit, and I know security is always watching."

"Observing is one thing. Response time is different."

As he would know. "Look, Kane—"

His eyes were filled with the same steely resolve they had been earlier when he stood up to Soren. "What's the harm in allowing me to be a gentleman?"

If he'd continued to assert his will, she would have responded in kind. But it was as if he knew her well enough already to back down and change his approach in order to win the battle. "You, sir, are more rogue than gentleman."

He shrugged. "My mom did her best with what she had."

It was one of the first things he'd revealed about himself. "Do you still have her?"

"After I joined the service, she moved to the coast. I see her when I can."

37

His arrogance might annoy her, but he did have old-world manners beneath his gruff, warrior exterior. "Well, I think she did a damn good job."

Kane tipped an imaginary hat in her direction. "When we talk, I'll be sure to pass along your words."

Did he mean that? "I accept your offer. Thank you."

He stood and assisted her up. Then after sanitizing the area, he knelt to help her slip back into her shoes.

Hand in hand, he walked her to the ladies' locker room and was waiting when she emerged wearing her flats and her coat with most of the buttons fastened.

Kane was wearing a jacket and had a black duffel embroidered with some sort of gold logo slung over his shoulder. His toy bag? And what did he bring with him to the club? Maybe she should have asked when he mentioned it earlier. Then a secondary thought floated through her mind. If he'd grabbed it, he was evidently leaving also, which meant he wouldn't be scening with any other women. She didn't want to think about why that realization made her so damn happy.

"Ready?"

She nodded.

They exited the dungeon into the much quieter reception area. Harmony called out a cheery good night while Soren folded his arms and silently watched them go.

"I'm in the closest parking lot." As she neared her vehicle, she glanced around, then pushed a button on the key fob to unlock the doors and start the engine.

"You pay attention to your surroundings. Keep doing that."

As earlier, when he expressed his approval, she drank it in and savored the sweetness.

He opened the driver's door.

Most definitely, he was a gentleman.

"If you'd like to scene again, contact me." He reached into

the side pocket of his bag and pulled out a business card that he handed to her.

It was emblazoned with the same design as his bag. Hawkeye. "I appreciate the offer." Her response was ambiguous, more suited to the old Morgan than the new, more assertive version. But she didn't want to come out and say, "No chance, Sir. If I call you once, I might never stop." Even though he was being polite, even solicitous right now, he was still the man who'd hurt her once.

She dropped his contact information into her pocket. "Thank you for a wonderful evening, Kane."

A smile teased his lips. "I was wondering when you'd remember to thank your Top. Or was that not covered in class?"

It had been. And regular manners dictated that she should have done so earlier. "I blame you."

"Ah." He tipped his head to one side, studying her. A streetlamp highlighted the interest in his eyes. "Do you?"

"What you did to me…" Morgan blew out a breath. "I'm not sure I could have remembered my own name."

"MJ."

"You're right. And I definitely wouldn't have recalled that." She laughed.

"I'm pleased."

"Thank you."

"You're more than welcome, sweetheart. I appreciate you letting me be your first. It's an evening I'll never forget, a memory I'll return to when I'm thousands of miles from home."

The reminder of what he did for a living sent a small shudder through her.

"Teasing aside, Kane, it was everything I could have hoped for."

"I'm pleased."

A breeze ruffled her already-out-of-control hair. And he slid errant strands behind her ears.

"I'd like to kiss you."

Once had almost destroyed her. Yet as she met his eyes, she could deny neither of them. "Yes."

He slanted his lips over hers. In an impossibly gentle manner, he sought entrance. For a man who mainlined adventure, and no doubt knew dozens of ways to kill a man, this tenderness was a paradox.

His tongue found hers, and she moaned, helplessly leaning into him, wrapping her arms around his neck in complete surrender.

Kane responded in kind, pressing one palm to that spot at the base of her spine and the other to the middle of her back. She was safe here, and it was as right as it was natural.

The kiss was long and slow, tasting of reassurance and a lingering sweetness from his beverage at the bar.

Right then, her phone rang, shattering the moment. She debated ignoring it. But at this time of the night, it might be important. Pulling back, she ended the kiss. "Sorry."

He nodded tightly. "I understand duty."

Maybe the interruption had been fortuitous, occurring before she had the chance to ask him to come home with her.

She opened her purse to dig out the cell phone and look at the phone screen. "My parents' dog sitter." Frowning, she answered, and a cacophony of barks drowned out the woman's frantic words. "Joyce? Tell the dogs *treats.*"

Moments later, there was blessed silence in the background. "Is everything okay?

"No." Fear laced the single word.

Next to her, evidently overhearing, Kane raised an interested eyebrow.

"What's going on?"

"I think… No. I'm sure…"

Trying to soothe and reassure, Morgan spoke responded. "Why don't you start at the beginning?"

"Okay. Okay." Joyce took a breath. "I took the dogs for their nighttime walk, and when we got back... The house wasn't like I left it."

What did that mean?

"A couple of items were moved, and...I'm not sure, but I think a few things are missing."

"Like what?" Morgan struggled to make sense of what she was hearing.

Kane leaned forward so as not to miss any of the conversation.

"This sounds ridiculous. There doesn't seem to be a break-in. I set the alarm when we left, and it was still that way when I returned. But certain things are different. My drink wasn't on a coaster. And... Morgan, there was a computer on your dad's desk, wasn't there? I'm sure there was. But now there's not."

Her stomach plummeted.

"I don't know if I should call the police."

Kane held up a finger to capture Morgan's attention.

She nodded her response, indicating she'd be with him in a second. "Joyce, hang tight. You know where the dog chews are, right?"

"In the pantry."

"May want to get them before they run out of patience." No doubt the animals were sensing Joyce's agitation.

The background sounds indicated Joyce was saying soothing things to the pups, and Morgan took the opportunity to press the mute button.

"I'll drive you to your parents' house."

"Wait. No. The house is in Parker." Which at least twenty to thirty minutes from here. "I'm sure I can figure things out." Even if she had no idea where to start. "But thank you for your offer."

"Sweetheart, you don't have a fucking clue what you're dealing with."

At the harshness of his tone and words, she brought her chin up, ready to do battle.

He sighed. "Sorry. I'll try again. Your dad has had a couple of stores robbed."

"I know that." Then his words registered. "You think this is connected?"

"Possibly."

"God." If this wasn't random, it was all the more terrifying. "Damn. I've gotta—" *Stay calm. Think and act rationally.*

Kane grabbed his own phone, punched a button, then took a few steps away. He spoke rapidly, giving someone a long explanation of what was going on.

Resolved, she returned to the call with the pet sitter.

"You're coming right? I don't feel safe here, and I don't want to stay. I'll take the dogs to my apartment just till you get here."

Not many people did have the room for four standard poodles and a rambunctious puppy. "Understood. Hang tight. I'm on my way."

"Okay." Her voice shaky, Joyce ended the call.

Morgan stood there, staring at the blank phone as Kane continued to give a clipped version of the events to the person on the other end of his phone.

When he rejoined her, he nodded tightly. "Let's go."

"Really, Kane—"

"Sweetheart, this is not a negotiation. I'm going with you."

His Dom voice was back, but rather than irritating her, this time she was reassured.

"It makes logical sense. Call Pierce from the road and

your parents, if you want. It'll be easier for you to focus if you're not driving."

His suggestions made sense.

"Where are your parents?"

"They went to New Orleans to take care of business. Then they decided to take a cruise since they were already there. But I can try to reach them."

Because she obviously wasn't thinking as straight as she wanted to be, he took the key fob from her and shut off the engine, closed and locked the doors, then escorted her to his big ass SUV that looked more like a tank than a car.

As if she weighed nothing at all, he lifted her onto the passenger seat, then reached across to fasten her seatbelt.

"Address?"

She gave it to him, and he repeated the information to his GPS system.

As they pulled out of the parking lot, she looked at him. She realized she was grateful to him. For all her words about being able to take care of herself, she was glad she didn't have to face this alone. "Thank you."

He looked at her. "Sweetheart, you may have already figured out that I'd do anything for you."

CHAPTER THREE

HAWKEYE

S *hit just got real.*

The scene with Morgan left Kane hot, turned-on, wanting to be buried deep in her hot pussy. And now there was a break-in at her parents' home. His years of fieldwork told him there was no way it wasn't related to the art case.

Now that he'd had her in his arms, over his lap, his hand on her bottom, marking her skin, and that long, slow-burn kiss, there was no way he was leaving her side.

He pulled out into the late evening traffic of downtown Denver and took a shortcut that would get him back to the highway faster.

Next to him the petite beauty picked up her phone once more and placed a call.

"You trying Pierce?" It was a guess.

She nodded.

Because they were seated so close together, he could overhear everything.

When she reached her brother's voicemail, she released a sigh of frustration.

"From what I know, he's at Hawkeye's remote training

center, out in the field on one of their survival exercises. He and a couple of guys are attempting to evade enemy fire, and they have no technology with them."

"I should be used to this with all the time he's spent deployed."

"When you have an emergency, it sucks."

She wrinkled her nose. Like right now. "I'll try my dad. Not that I expect to get him."

Surprising her, he answered on the first ring.

She dug her fingernails into her palms as she gave a quick synopsis of the situation, ending with, "I'm going to contact the police."

"Don't do that," her father snapped.

Meeting Kane's eyes, she frowned.

Interesting. That was the reaction Kane expected from someone with something to hide. Keep law enforcement as far away from the situation as possible.

"I think I should call them." When he didn't respond, Morgan pressed forward. "What if someone is still there?"

"Don't be ridiculous Morgan. Would you fucking use your head?"

Who in the hell does this man think he is? Kane extended his hand for the phone.

Frantically she shook her head.

"Give it to me." When she didn't, he took the phone from her.

"Don't you ever goddamn well talk to your daughter like that again. Are we clear?"

Morgan's mouth fell open as she gasped.

"Who the fuck are you?"

"Kane Patterson, former US Army, currently employed by Hawkeye and taking care of Morgan."

"So you're another one of *them.*" Derision dripped from

Holden's tone. "Always skulking as if the bogeyman is out to get you."

Kane's tenuous hold on his temper began to unravel. "Listen, you disrespectful bastard. When you're back in town, we will have a discussion. Now unless you want to treat Morgan with a little more civility, this call is over." His next words were a calculated gamble. "I'll back any damn play she wants to make."

Morgan shrank back into her seat.

Maybe it wasn't his place—probably wasn't, a saner part of his brain recognized—and she might not thank him for it, but he would not stand by and allow anyone to treat his woman that way.

His woman?

When had he started thinking of her in those terms? And so fast, as if it was natural.

He slid her a glance. Her earlier protests about not wanting his protection no longer mattered to him—if they ever did. Whether she was willing to admit it or not, Morgan Holden—*his* MJ—was now under his protection. It was a job he took seriously.

In this moment, his personal and professional lives were inextricably woven together. He and Morgan were in this for the long haul. No matter what that meant or looked like.

Kane refocused on the conversation. "Would you like to try again, Mr. Holden?"

"Put my daughter back on."

"You received a warning from me. First and last." With that clarified, Kane offered the device back to Morgan.

Since she didn't adjust the call volume, Kane was privy to every word.

"Joyce is probably overreacting. You know how she is."

"Did you leave your computer at home?"

"Yes," Holden responded with an exasperated huff.

"It's gone. And, well, I think you'll need a police report for an insurance claim?"

Another of the man's annoyed sighs reached across the thousands of miles. "I won't be filing a claim. My fingerprint is needed to unlock it, and everything is backed up to the Bonds cloud service. At best, someone got away with a used piece of equipment that's no good to them. And they couldn't hack into it if they tried."

That made sense, but there was the lingering detail of the break-in. "What about the alarm being bypassed? Doesn't that bother you?"

"Joyce is mistaken. Forgot to turn it on and is covering up her mistake."

She held the phone away from her for a minute and looked at it, as if disbelieving this discussion was real. "You should have gotten an alert on the doorbell camera, right?"

"I didn't. Look, Morgan, let it go. It's probably just kids wanting some extra money. Your mother told me the neighborhood watch group says it's happening a lot. Stop being such a worrier. Let me know if you actually find anything important at the house. I'm sure everything's fine."

The man is a piece of shit.

She'd expressed her fears that someone might be in the home, and her father brushed off everything, made it seem like a figment of her imagination, and didn't care if she went in alone.

Someone had been in the house. So why the fuck would the older Mr. Holden dismiss the truth and pretend nothing happened?

More than ever, Kane was glad he was with her.

With a deep sigh, she dropped her phone back into her purse.

Primly, in an action he now recognized as an attempt to cover her nerves, she folded her hands in her lap.

48

"I don't understand what's going on here." As she faced him, her eyes were wide.

Unfortunately there wasn't enough ambient light for him to decipher her expression. "Do you want my guess?" He'd already told her she had no idea what she was dealing with. He wasn't sure he fully comprehended, either, but he had a better idea than she did.

"Yes."

"Police aren't always the best recourse." That probably wasn't an adequate explanation. "At the most, they'll take a report, as you suggested. They're busy. Overworked." At times lazy. "Unless there's a sign of a forced entry"—and even if there was—"they're unlikely to send out a crime scene team. Unless a lot more is missing than Joyce realized, we're talking petty theft. Not worth prosecuting."

"Honestly I'd feel better if someone went in with me."

He suppressed his smile. Most likely he'd drawn a gun more times than any member of local law enforcement, including their Emergency Services Team. "Hawkeye agents will be there before we are. They'll…" He paused. *Secure the site.* Dealing with civilians wasn't his strong suit. For her, he'd damn well try. It wasn't a site to her. It was her parents' home—somewhere that was supposed to be a place of refuge. "Make sure you're safe."

"If what Pierce says is true, Hawkeye Security is the best. Probably better than cops?"

"Yeah." He slid her a glance. "I tend to agree with that."

"I'm sure you would."

"No false modesty. Our teams are composed of former law enforcement, including covert CIA and FBI operatives." And ones from another dozen or so agencies, all bearing various acronyms he could no longer keep straight. "We've got a lot of military guys—and women—also. And everyone goes through advanced training at our facility in Nevada."

"I know I said this once, but I really am glad you're with me. Sorry that I'm ruining the rest of your Saturday night."

"Sweetheart, there's no place I'd rather be."

"Danger is something you feed on?"

"Lifeblood." And he'd walk through fire to be with her.

"I'm going to try Pierce again."

He recognized what she was doing, even if she didn't. Taking an action, any action, so she didn't feel helpless.

When the call went straight to voicemail as expected, he pushed a button on his dashboard. Seconds later, his summons was answered.

"Inamorata."

Morgan turned in his direction.

"Holden needs to call his sister. It's an emergency."

"Acknowledged."

The screen went blank, and silence once again filled the car's interior.

"Who, or what, was that?"

"Hawkeye's right-hand person."

"There really is a Hawkeye? It's not just the name of a company?"

"He's very real, I assure you." And shadowy as fuck. "Inamorata keeps the organization running smoothly and handles logistics." How she kept such a dizzying array of details straight, he had no idea. Most likely, she never slept.

"I think you were right earlier. There's something going on I don't have any idea about."

"Yeah."

"But she can get in contact with Pierce, even though he's in the field?"

"A message will be relayed to the safety-support crew."

"Thank you." As her mind sifted through reams of information, she fell silent for a moment. "You mentioned the break-ins at the Dallas stores and that they might be connected."

He didn't bother answering.

"How did you know that?"

A week ago, Hawkeye had told Logan that giving Pierce information was on a need-to-know basis, so Kane chose his words with care. "Months ago, we were hired by an insurance agency after some of their clients had been robbed. Art pieces and some jewelry."

"I see."

No doubt she did. *But how clearly?*

AS THEY EXITED the highway at Lincoln, her phone rang.

After glancing at the screen, she sighed. "Joyce again. I don't even have a clue what to say."

"You're doing your best."

It didn't seem to be enough, though.

Forcing herself to be calm, she answered, and Joyce immediately started speaking.

"When will you be here? My downstairs neighbor saw me and threatened to call management about the dogs."

"I promise I'll handle it as soon as I can." And add several hundred dollars extra to her tip. "I apologize."

"I'll bring them over if you want."

"Let me make sure things are safe first."

"The babies have never acted like this before."

"They're amazingly perceptive, aren't they? Anyway, I'll update you as soon as I can. Promise." She ended the call. How had her life gotten so out of control in under an hour?

"Sounds as if she has her hands full."

"She's really good with them, and that's why Mom trusts her. But she's rattled. And at the best of times, the five of them can be a lot to handle."

"Five? Good God."

"My mom has been getting a new one every year, and my dad is not a fan. I think she mostly does it to annoy him."

"I can see how that would accomplish her mission."

Morgan appreciated the conversation. It kept her from worrying about the things that were momentarily beyond her control. "You're not an animal lover?"

"No objection to them in general. But I've never had a pet, so I have no idea."

Morgan waited for him to go on.

"Grew up in a small home. My mom would have had one if my dad would have agreed. Now she has two somewhat badly behaved Pomeranians."

"I love those. They're smart, great companions." She smiled. "I like your mother already."

"You'll have to meet her."

He was having a casual conversation, not planning a future. Or at least that's what she told herself. Soon, he'd be leaving again.

The app screen on his dashboard lit up, and Inamorata's name appeared on the display. He tapped the icon to read the message.

Team is in place.

A result of the call he'd placed earlier?

That he wasn't being secretive took her aback. Her ex had always been hiding something, and her father operated in the shadows. So she appreciated Kane's transparency. "That was fast."

"Sometimes I'm even astounded by how quickly she operates."

Standby for sitrep.

"Sitrep?" She looked at him.

"A situation report. Inamorata will shoot us a preliminary update within a couple of minutes."

Right at the moment where they turned off a major street onto a dirt road and in a place where cell signal was notoriously bad, Pierce called. Inamorata was amazing.

Morgan answered straight away.

"I've been advised of the situation."

Of course he had been.

"Kane Patterson is with you?"

She glanced at the hardened, competent man in the driver's seat, the one shamelessly eavesdropping on every word she said. "He is."

"I'll vouch for him. Take his advice." Thank God he hadn't asked why she was with Kane on a Saturday night.

"Dad doesn't want me to call the police."

He was silent for so long that she checked to be sure they were still connected.

"We'll let it play out."

"What does that mean?" Did every man in her life talk in shorthand that only they understood.

"Don't call them. You can always do so later if necessary."

Before she could say anything else, the call dropped.

"I feel like Alice—you know the one from the movie."

"Wonderland?" he suggested. "As in you've fallen down a rabbit hole?"

"How do you do this all the time?"

When he glanced at her without answering, she clarified her words. "I mean, a hundred moving parts at the same time. Things that don't make sense?"

"Second nature. Wouldn't say I'm okay with unanswered questions, but I look for patterns, things that don't fit. Connections. In the end, most of it makes sense." He shrugged. "Not always. There can be losses that can be hard to swallow."

Which might be why she preferred to stick to marketing. There was a puzzle to it. Certain things worked better than others, but she could always analyze the data she received and work it into the next idea.

"Only thing that rattles me is if the people I care about are threatened." He fell quiet for a moment. "You, for example."

Seriously?

"So when we arrive, please do as I say with no arguments."

She blinked.

"As I said—"

"You are who you are."

"No apology." He'd compromise nothing to ensure her safety.

Premises and perimeter secure.

There was definitely no way the local police department could have handled all of this so quickly.

They turned onto her parents' street.

His grip on the steering wheel was light but competent, not betraying any of the tension racing through her.

"I meant it earlier; I'm glad you're with me."

"Wouldn't have allowed you to handle this alone."

"What if I gave you no choice?"

"I'd have followed you. Or called HQ for the address."

The house came into view. Lights blazed from the windows, but there was no sign of any vehicles or people. "Did the Hawkeye people leave already?"

"No. They're around."

"Where?" She saw…nothing.

He braked to a stop in the driveway. "That's the *secret* part of your secret agent quip."

His joke was terrible, but it helped keep tension at bay.

Before she could exit the vehicle, he was there to help her down. "I'm going to need a step ladder to get in and out of this machine."

"Not as long as you've got me."

He swung her out and gently placed her down. For a second, he held her. And she wanted to stay there forever.

"Ready?"

Not ever.

He cupped her elbow as they walked to the backdoor where she keyed in the code to turn off the alarm system.

When they entered the house, she froze. Two people—a man and a woman—were standing behind the kitchen island.

"They're friendlies," Kane reassured her.

After closing the door, she turned to reset the alarm—for all the good that would do her. If Joyce was correct, someone had managed to get in without tripping it, and so did the Hawkeye agents. Unless Pierce gave them the code. She'd be surprised, however, if her dad had given it to him. And the fact her father hadn't called upset that people were in his kitchen proved that they'd entered without the doorbell camera being activated. "This is supposedly all a state-of-the-art system."

"No doubt it is."

"So…?" She was confused.

"Criminals are masterminds." He shrugged. "And the good guys know a thing or two also."

"How do you tell the two apart?"

"There's a thin line, depending on which side you're on. Allow me to perform the introductions. Morgan Holden, Ms. Inamorata." The woman was well put together in high-heeled pumps, and a slim-fitting pencil skirt. Despite the late hour on a Saturday night, her makeup was impeccable, and she didn't have a single strand of hair out of place.

The woman strode toward her to shake her hand. "Sorry we had to meet under these circumstances."

"I'm in awe of what you've accomplished."

Kane introduced the man as Logan Powell. "The team leader heading up investigations into a few break-ins."

At Kane's description, Logan raised an eyebrow before nodding toward her. "Ma'am. Your brother's a friend of mine. Has been for a long time."

"We've met."

"Ma'am?"

"At Joe and Noelle's wedding. It was a long time ago, but I was a bridesmaid."

"Ah." There was no light of recognition in his eyes. "Jennifer, your fiancée, is one of my friends."

"You're a member of the Carpe Diem Divas?"

She attempted a smile. "I'm sure our reputation is overexaggerated."

"I'll have her call you. Once she knows I've seen you, she'll be worried about you and dying of curiosity."

How was it possible that she'd felt isolated at the club, and now a group of people were closing around her, trying to be helpful?

Logan's phone chimed, and he stepped away to take the call.

Even from across the room, she recognized the sound of her brother's voice but not the no-nonsense, clipped tone. "What the fuck is going on out there?"

"I know this has to be uncomfortable…" Inamorata gave a half smile which Morgan imagined was about as much as she displayed compassion. "Do you have any idea who could have done this? Or why?"

"I wish I did."

"It would be helpful if you could perhaps walk through the house, room by room, to let us know if there's anything out of the ordinary."

"I don't know how much use I can be. As you know, I don't live here, and when I visit, I mostly stay in the kitchen or sit outside with my mom."

"Still, you're the best resource we have right now."

That much was true. Wrapping her arms around herself against the chill, she glanced around. As Joyce noted on the phone, her drink was not on its coaster. Remnants from dog treats were scattered across the floor. If her mother were home, she'd be aghast and demanding the housekeeping service show up first thing in the morning.

On the counter were a set of blueprints for the pool and guest quarters her mother was hoping to build. Laurel had been hoping that her son would visit more often if he had a nice place to stay that wasn't in the main house. But now that he was planning a life with Ella, that was even less likely than it had been before.

As she shuffled through the elaborate sketches, she could almost hear her father's voice as if he were in the room. *"We can't afford that, dear."*

And then her mother's syrupy sweet response, *"Make it happen, Gerry."*

Beneath the papers was a signed contract with building slated to begin in less than two weeks.

"Something out of the ordinary, Ms. Holden?" Inamorata asked.

Like Kane, she missed nothing.

"Probably not. Mom's been wanting a pool and accompanying guesthouse for a long time, but I had no idea she signed a contract." And the price was at least triple what she'd told her father it would cost.

"May I?"

Morgan turned over the contract. "Does the price seem excessive to you?"

"A million dollars? Yes."

Kane held out his hand, and Inamorata turned over the contract.

The next stop was her father's study. His new, sleek Bonds computer was not where he generally left it. She

57

looked in drawers and in the credenza, even the closet, but it was nowhere around.

Inamorata had accompanied her in. "Anything besides the laptop?"

"Not that I can see." She was aware that Kane was still nearby, quiet, strong.

Logan returned, offering his phone to her. "Your brother would like a word."

None of the Hawkeye team budged to give her privacy. Kane definitely fit in with them. Turning her back to them, she wandered to the window and stared out. The people in the room were visible in the reflection. And she wondered if anyone was outside looking at her. The thought unnerved her. No wonder Joyce had gotten the hell out of here.

"Morgan?"

"Yeah. I'm here. Did you know Mom signed a contract on the expansion project? I found the paperwork beneath the sketches, like she was hiding them or something."

"I never talk to them. But it seems Dad's not the only one who does shady things."

"Still want me to keep the police out of it?"

"For now. Even if you call them, Dad can immediately close the case by saying he had his laptop with him. And say Joyce forgot to set the alarm and lied to cover it up. Nothing but a big misunderstanding, sorry for your inconvenience, and by the way, here's a donation to the police benevolent fund."

She could picture their dad using those exact words, and he definitely believed money solved all issues and greased plenty of wheels.

"Call if you need anything."

Not that he would answer.

After returning the phone to Logan, they all continued

the room-by-room sweep of the house. This was so surreal as to be fantastical.

Once they finished with the main level, she led the way to the second floor.

Pierce's room had largely remained untouched since the day he eternally pissed off their father by enlisting in the military. Now it was part shrine, part moment frozen in time.

"Damn." Logan whistled.

His reaction was an echo of her thoughts.

All the surfaces had a layer of dust on them. How long had it been since their mom had allowed the housekeepers inside the space? Maybe since she'd had it cleaned in hopes he'd stay at the home when he was last here for their thirtieth wedding anniversary celebration.

Thank God her mother had hired a decorator to update her room. Still, she was ultra-aware of Kane taking in the deep rich colors and the nine pillows.

He cast a glance at the bed, and then their gazes met. She couldn't help her body's automatic response, and she knew she was turning a dozen shades of scarlet.

Afraid Inamorata and Logan would know what she and Kane had been doing—despite the fact they were grown-ass adults—she looked away and tightened the belt around her waist, remembering she was wearing a scandalously short dress.

Next was the guest room where everything appeared to be in order.

But as she entered her parents' massive suite, she intuitively recognized that something was off.

Then it hit her. Her mom's nightstand was typically laden with framed snapshots of the dogs—from shows, wearing ribbons, or dressed in their holiday finery with Santa or the Easter Bunny.

"Morgan?" Inamorata asked.

"I'm not sure." She walked to the nightstand. Only one picture remained, and it had been turned facedown.

She reached for it.

"Please don't touch it," Inamorata said.

Kane clamped his hand on her wrist. She blinked at him. "What's going on?"

"Tell us what you see."

While she interacted with Kane, Logan started taking pictures with his cell phone.

"I… It's usually filled with photos. Unless Mom took them to New Orleans with her."

"Is that a possibility?" Inamorata asked.

Slowly Kane released her, and she stepped back so she didn't give into the temptation of reaching for the frame again. Which picture had been left behind? And why wasn't it standing up like it usually was?

"When it comes to her babies, I don't rule anything out. I mean, she has hundreds, maybe thousands of photos of them on her phone." And perhaps one of her and Pierce together. "Last time I remember being in here, the nightstand was jam-packed with pictures. There wasn't even room for a lamp."

Inamorata nodded toward Logan, who pulled out a pair of nitrile gloves from a pocket inside his Hawkeye jacket.

Who kept those kind of supplies with them?

She really had fallen down a rabbit hole.

Taking great care, he turned over the photo. It was a new one that Laurel had commissioned—the first professional shot of all five dogs together.

"Mind if we take it?" Inamorata asked.

She blinked.

"They'll get it back as soon as possible, hopefully before your parents return." Kane's voice was reassuring. "If it's not back in time, your mother will assume it's missing with the others."

"There has to be a reason it was left like that, right?"

"Or someone dropped it, didn't have the room, got spooked. Any number of possibilities exist."

What Kane said made sense, so she nodded.

"Bag it."

At Inamorata's instruction, Logan pulled out a large see-through plastic bag.

"What are you wearing? A magician's cape?"

"Hazard of the job." Logan chuckled.

She glanced at Kane. Was he carrying all kinds of things in his jacket also?

Logan used a permanent marker to label the contents and added the word *RUSH*.

"Is that necessary? Mom will have a fit that it's missing." What was she saying? All the others were gone too.

Kane took over the explanation. "We're looking for fingerprints."

"What about the security system? Dad's desk? The glass Joyce was drinking out of?"

"Team has already lifted the evidence."

Damn, Hawkeye Security moved fast.

When they were back in the kitchen, Inamorata spoke again. "Almost done."

Almost?

"Sorting through all the prints will take a while, and we'll need to match the ones that belong here. I need a list of people who you think might have access to the house."

It was more order than request.

"Joyce, of course."

Inamorata pulled out her phone and slid out the stylus. "Last name?"

She provided the information. "Pierce, but he hasn't been here for a while. Me. The housekeepers."

"A person or a service?"

"Happy Spaces, though they generally send out the same team."

"Anyone else?"

"I don't know. Not off the top of my head."

"If you think of anybody else, let us know."

Her phone rang again. She checked the screen. "It's my dad."

"Mind if we stay in the room?"

Why bother objecting? No doubt they'd surreptitiously listen, regardless.

And she had no doubt Kane would remain even if she told him to leave. The way he'd spoken to her father still shocked her. In her life, no one had ever championed her before.

After a breath, she answered. "Hi, Dad. So I'm at the house. I didn't find your computer."

He cursed. "Damn kids."

"And... Did Mom bring any pictures of the babies with her?"

"Good God no. With all her clothes and cosmetics, there was no room. Why do you ask?"

Since she didn't want her dad and mom to know she'd snooped through their house with an entire team of people, but wanting to confirm the pictures had been there when they left, she tried for a quick cover story. "I was hoping to see the new one she's been raving about—the best one from the professional shoot."

"It's on her nightstand, but there's no reason for you to go in our room."

There was a strange sound in the background—maybe a door slamming. "Back from the casino so soon, darling?"

All of a sudden, her mother was on the phone. *"My babies! My poor precious babies!"* Laurel's words slurred. She had clearly had a steady supply of mimosas today.

"It's okay, Mom. Right now they're safe at Joyce's."

"No!" Laurel wailed the word. "You know they can't be away from home."

Morgan barely resisted the impulse to roll her eyes. "They'll be back soon."

"But what then?"

Morgan had no clue. "Joyce is nervous about being over at your house, so I doubt she's planning to come back tomorrow, and she isn't allowed to have pets at her place."

"I can't bear the fact someone was in my home and upset my babies."

Which is the bigger concern? And she was so worried that she went to the casino?

"Gerry, book us a flight home from the Caribbean tomorrow. Morgan, promise them that Mommy will be home tomorrow."

In the background, her father was trying to speak over his wife. "Nothing we can do there, darling. We might as well enjoy ourselves."

"Gerry! You're a beast. These are my babies we're talking about."

"I'm sure they're fine, darling."

As always, Morgan was a silent witness to the dramatics between her mother and father. "Put the phone on speaker, Mom." She was tired of the ping-pong conversation, and she had plenty to say that both of them needed to hear. "Look, Dad, Mom's right. She needs to be with them. Joyce isn't available, and I can't watch them."

"What? Why can't you take care of the babies?" Laurel demanded, the sobs suddenly gone from her voice.

"I need to be at my condo, and I have a job."

"Take time off. Your father is fine with it."

Morgan closed her eyes. "I'm not. I have a life of my own."

Near her, Kane silently clapped.

Maybe she should be more like Pierce, refusing to be sucked into their reality. "If you don't want to come home, fine. I'll board the dogs at the vet's office."

Laurel gasped, then shrieked. "You're a beast like your father."

"The vet's it is." Exasperated, she ended the call and dropped her phone back into her purse.

A moment later, the reality of the ridiculous discussion knocked the breath out of her. Neither of her parents had asked how she was. Not that it should surprise her. She'd grown up this way. In retrospect, it made sense that she fought in every way she knew how to get her needs met in her previous relationship.

She didn't apologize for the way her parents had behaved. All the Hawkeye operatives had opted to stay and listen to the exchange.

"If you think of anything that might be useful, or if you need anything, don't hesitate to reach out. Night or day." From a pocket on the back of her cell phone, Inamorata pulled out a business card and offered it to Morgan.

She took it and dropped it into her pocket alongside Kane's.

"Someone will be in touch if we learn anything."

Never mind the fact she'd given no one her number.

"I trust Kane will be sure you have a ride home." The woman smiled.

"Ms. Holden is safe with me."

Logan regarded him but said nothing.

She disarmed the security system, and in less than a minute she was alone with Kane, the house preternaturally quiet now that everyone was gone.

She expelled a breath and realized her hands were trembling.

"You've been through a lot."

And there was still the pack to think about. "I need to get in contact with Joyce. If we need to go and get the dogs, you're definitely going to be sorry you insisted on bringing your car."

"I've seen combat. It can't be worse."

She smiled. "He said bravely."

Before she could finish sending the text, Joyce pulled into the driveway.

"I'll meet her outside."

Without a word, he followed.

In a testament to how shaken Joyce was, collars and leashes were not color coordinated. She made no attempt to get the animals to behave. And Bella, the littlest princess, squatted to pee all over the concrete. All of the dogs barked and dashed around. If this kept up, her neighbors would be complaining as well.

"I need to take a Valium."

"I'm so sorry you went through all this." She dug a generous tip from her bag.

"Keep it. I quit. You can't pay me enough to put up with anymore of this shit."

"Joyce, at least—"

Without waiting for her to finish her sentence the woman climbed back into her car and pulled out of the driveway so fast that her wheels spun.

One of the dogs, maybe Fifi, jumped up on Kane. "I'm so sorry." She pulled on the leash.

But instead of reacting badly, he scratched the pooch behind its ears.

The dog's tongue lolled out in total happiness.

"I need to get them under control."

"Can I help?"

The leashes were a tangled disaster, and right now this ranked up there with herding kittens. "Get the door?"

Once they were inside, she unclipped each dog, starting with Walter, the alpha, and ending with Bella.

Now that they were free, they dashed through the house, sniffing everything. No wonder Joyce had given up in frustration.

But now the rest of the evening loomed. What was she going to do about the pups until tomorrow?

Kane opened the refrigerator and pulled out a bottle of wine. "Mind if I open it?"

"If you don't, I will." And she didn't care how expensive it was. "Corkscrew is in that drawer." While he busied himself, she grabbed two glasses, and he poured a generous amount into each.

He lifted his glass toward hers, and she clinked it. After a fortifying drink, she leaned against the counter, letting it take all her weight.

"We need to make a plan."

"We?"

"Of course."

"That's sweet of you." His coming to the club tonight had been a lifesaver. "I can't thank you enough for everything. I've already taken up too much of your time."

"What are you doing with the dogs tonight?"

"My living situation is no better than Joyce's." She sighed wearily.

"Oh?"

"I live in a high-rise."

"No yard for them to run or play?" he guessed.

Yet the idea of staying here made her uncomfortable, especially since the home had been burglarized without setting off the alarm. Even her mom had accidentally tripped it on numerous occasions.

"So as I see it, there are two options. You and I can stay here where the dogs are comfortable with all their pillows and blankets and crates. Toys. Food. Bowls."

As they'd moved through the house, he'd been observant.

"Moving them would be a monumental task. Who the hell knew they needed so much stuff?"

"Wait until you see the garage with leashes, harness, collars, and the dresser filled with holiday sweaters."

"Clothing? Actual garments?" He blinked. "You're not joking?"

"Not even a little bit. I'll bet your mom has some for her Pomeranians." She grinned as he shuddered.

"Perish the thought."

She took another sip and allowed the cool drink to soothe her.

"There's a team onsite. The house is as secure as Fort Knox."

Tension she hadn't realized she'd been holding onto eased from her shoulders.

"But you also have a second choice."

"Oh?"

"You and the fabulous five can come to my house."

The choices he'd given her were impossible.

"What will it be, sweetheart?"

CHAPTER FOUR

HAWKEYE

She exhaled.

As usual, Kane was right—this time about her options.

A quick glance at the wall clock said it was already after eleven, and in the last few minutes, the dogs had started to settle down. No doubt that was due in part to Kane's presence that kept her calm. Without him, she'd be restless, unable to sit still for more than five minutes.

They would need time to load up the dogs. And even though he drove a massive SUV, she doubted the whole pack, and all their belongings and kennels, would fit inside. Even if he lived nearby, it would be at least midnight before everyone was settled.

If he was right about the house being secure, the best option was to remain here.

"We're staying? Your face is telling me what I need to know, but I want to confirm it."

"That's what makes the most sense."

"Agree."

Even though her heart wasn't in it, and guilt at what she

was putting him through assailed her, she looked across the kitchen at him. "You've done so much for me tonight. I understand if you need to go."

"Sweetheart, there's no chance of me walking away. Not ever again."

His sense of responsibility awed her. That's what it was, she reminded herself. Nothing more.

"Since you've reached a decision, why don't you finally take off that coat?" His voice was a bit more dangerous now.

She smiled. With everything else that had happened since they left the Reserve, that was the last thing on her mind.

After placing her glass on the counter behind her, she loosened the knot in her belt, then unfastened the buttons.

He never took his hungry eyes off her.

Finally she shrugged out of the garment.

Like he had at the club, he slowly perused her. Then he smiled. "Sweetheart, maybe you should put it back on."

Even though he was nowhere close to touching her, her body warmed as if he had.

She walked to the table where she draped the coat over the back of a chair.

Aware of his gaze on her, she tugged down the hem of the dress. Now she wished she had something other than club-wear in her bag or a change of clothes in her room.

Then it occurred to her that he might want to be more comfortable too. "Can I take your jacket for you?"

"Thanks." He removed it and handed it to her. "You'll want to be careful."

The thing was surprisingly heavy.

Then reality dawned in slow measures. "You have a gun in there?"

"In a built-in holster, yes. Safety is on, so you're not at any risk."

"How deep does this rabbit hole actually go?" *Does it even have a bottom?*

After carefully placing the jacket on a hook, she squared her shoulders, then returned to the kitchen to pick up her wine so she had something to occupy her hands.

"Let's go in the great room."

That had to be less awkward than standing here.

The dogs followed them, and Bon Bon hopped onto a chair that he wasn't supposed to be on. But she didn't have the heart—or energy—to move him.

She curled up onto the far end of the couch. Her dress left her so exposed that she picked up a pillow and placed it in her lap.

Kane, acting as if he'd been here a hundred times before, sat near her. Not right next to her, but close enough that he filled her senses.

"How can you be so comfortable here? If I were in some stranger's house, I wouldn't be as relaxed." Even though she'd grown up here, she was never completely at ease.

"Practice. In order to be my best, I need two things: rest and food. The military teaches you to do both when you can. Your brother has probably said something similar."

He hadn't. Pierce kept to himself about his way of life. She appreciated this glimpse that Kane was giving her.

"I've slept on the dirt floor of a hut in Africa. In a bunk in Iraq with mortar shells exploding. In a commandeered Middle Eastern neighborhood where insurgents could bomb us to hell and back." He grinned. "But to your point, sometimes suburbia is worse than that."

She took a sip of wine and studied him. "You mean being in someone else's home? Where they don't know you're hanging out. My dad, for example?"

"Him?" He waved a hand. "He doesn't bother me in the least."

Gerard Holden rattled her plenty. If he ever found out she'd allowed others to go through his house and that she'd happily accepted Kane's offer to stay with her, there'd be hell to pay.

"He's a bully. And needs to be stopped."

"I still can't believe you did that." *Took her phone and told the man to be respectful.*

"Don't expect an apology. No one deserves to be spoken to like that. And it won't be tolerated when I'm around."

She couldn't help but ask… "You'd do that for anyone?"

"No."

His response slowed her pulse.

"You're different." He paused. "Special."

But she wasn't either of those things.

"What your mother said about you taking time off. Do you work for your father?"

"I wouldn't necessarily say that." Much to her disappointment. She recognized the truth. Her father would never allow her anywhere near the C-suite at Holden International. If she wanted to take her career to the top, she'd have to look for a new position. "I work in marketing at the corporate headquarters downtown. But as far as having any association with my dad? No." She shook her head. "He doesn't think women are smart enough to run his company."

"He's an idiot."

She knew that, but even if she hadn't believed that, her mind would have been changed after seeing Inamorata in action. "He's been holding out hope that Pierce will quit playing war games and go to business school so he can take over when my dad retires."

"Knowing him, there's a better chance of hell freezing over."

"Absolutely."

"Your father seems shortsighted, especially given the fact your brother has no interest in the business."

"Dad thinks I should find a nice man and get married. He's hoping I'll produce a son who could become his heir."

"Jesus." Kane winced. "He really is a dinosaur."

"So… The dynamics are complicated. You don't really want to hear all this."

"Yeah." He plucked the now-empty wineglass from her grip. "I do."

Shamelessly she tracked him as he returned to the kitchen and refilled both drinks. Every movement was economical and competent, and he took a moment to check his phone. Always on duty?

He rejoined her, and she accepted the beverage. Already she was relaxing a little, and she was grateful. If he wasn't here, she probably would have spent the entire night on edge.

"If he doesn't have a change of heart, or if you don't deliver his requisite grandson, what's he going to do?"

"We've talked in vague terms about his succession planning, and my guess is he'll start grooming Harold Loughton." Realizing he had no idea who she meant, she explained. "Harold's dad and my father were originally in business together. And now Harold is the VP of Accounting."

"What happened to the partnership?"

She frowned, trying to recall. "You know, I have no idea. I understand they had disagreements about the future of the corporation. To my knowledge, Dad kept some parts. Harold's father got others. I guess it was mostly amicable; otherwise I'd remember, right? And why else would Harold be one of my dad's VPs if there was bad blood? The only thing I've ever heard is that he went with the person he thought was the better businessman."

"Is Harold still close with his father?"

Another good question. "We don't talk much. Since we're

in different departments, on separate floors, we don't have a lot of contact with each other. And the accounting people never want our marketing team to have all the money we need."

"Budget issues. Isn't that the way it always plays out in corporations?"

"Seems to be."

When she fell silent again, he quietly spoke. "I noticed that neither of your parents asked how you were doing."

"Why would they?" She attempted a half smile. "I mean, neither one of them seem concerned about the break-in. If it happened at all. Dad seems to think Joyce forgot to set the alarm, and that the theft is the work of teenagers."

"It wasn't. You know the truth. So do I."

"They don't know about the photos yet, though."

"Probably have an excuse for that as well."

No doubt he was right.

"Your mom was concerned about the dogs."

"They're her whole life."

"But neither of them asked if you were okay."

He was certainly persistent. Seeking a deeper answer? "I'm used to it."

Studying her deeply, he asked, "Does anyone get accustomed to that kind of callous treatment?"

Or had the hurt piled up so high that she was now numb to it? She stared into the bottom of her glass. "Maybe not."

"Let me be the one to ask. How *are* you doing?"

"I'm not even sure how to answer that to be honest. Tired. Really damn confused about everything." She leaned forward to slide her drink onto the coffee table, then rubbed her bare arms.

"Cold?"

It was more mental than physical, she was sure. Even though it was early fall, the house was plenty warm.

He stood to cross to the gas fireplace and flicked a nearby switch. Roaring flames sprung to life.

When he returned to his seat, he regarded her in silence. Giving her the space to talk if she wanted? "It's a lot to take in," she eventually said.

"And now that the adrenaline has subsided?"

"Is that what I'm feeling?"

"Could be. You were reacting to the moment as it unfolded. You went from a BDSM scene and its aftermath where you almost fell asleep…"

That seemed as if it had happened a lifetime ago.

"To Joyce's full-on panic and trying to figure out what was going on. You had decisions to make, logistics problems to solve, calls to make, and you were trying to keep Joyce calm. Then you had people in the house and dozens of questions lobbed at you. My guess is your senses have been on high alert for hours. But that state is not sustainable, and a crash is inevitable. Maybe you're more tired than you were before?"

"I actually feel alert, and my mind is spinning."

"Makes sense." He nodded. "You're someplace you can breathe deep, catch your breath."

This was a way of life for him. Definitely not for her. " Nothing about tonight makes sense. Does it to you?"

"Talk me through it. Sometimes things make more sense that way."

"You know as much, if not more, than I do, and you've seen it all unfold."

"True."

As an outside observer, he had a different perspective that she needed. "I believe Joyce."

"So do I."

"Not just because of the laptop, the picture, her glass being moved…" She stared into the fire. "How was the alarm bypassed? Why did my dad have so many excuses? If I thought someone had been in my house, I'd be far more concerned."

Finding a little energy again, she picked up her wineglass. "And the only things missing are the computer, which, like Dad says, may have little value—"

"If he's telling the truth."

She'd never considered him a liar. But at this point, anything was possible.

"Go on."

"And the photographs—except for the one that was face-down. Maybe I've listened to too many true-crime podcasts, but that feels personal to me."

He remained silent.

"Like someone is trying to send a message." She shuddered. "A warning or something." Now she was scaring herself.

He scooted closer and drew her against him to drape an arm around her shoulders.

She angled herself to look up at him. "What do you know that you haven't said?"

"Not much."

"You warned me that I had no clue what I was getting into. I think it's time you enlightened me."

"You probably know most of it, and I'm new to this team, so I'm not up to speed. But you can chat with Logan if you want."

She might. "Tell me what you do know." Maybe a random piece of information would help her understand.

"Since February—maybe a month or two earlier—there have been a number of art heists."

"I haven't heard of any in the news."

"None of them have been at major institutions and nothing that could be construed as a masterpiece. Most of the works are known to collectors only. Expensive? Yes. Priceless? No. Items that are easy to move or fence. At this point, law enforcement and insurance companies have not made their searches public."

"Is that normal?"

"As far as I know." He leaned forward for his own glass. "It's been about two months since the last incident."

"So...? They—whoever they are—got what they wanted? Made enough money?"

"Your guess is as good as mine. But in all cases, alarms were bypassed. No forced entry. Grab and go. No destruction of other property. The thieves knew what they were after and didn't get distracted. The operation has been surgical in its precision."

Despite the warmth and his touch, his quiet assessment brought her fear back in a terrible rush. "So you think what happened here is connected?"

"Don't jump to conclusions. I'm not saying it is."

"But you say you look for patterns. This seems to fit with everything else you've told me."

"Doesn't necessarily mean anything."

Still, she couldn't shake her sense of discomfort. Needing to do something, she stood and placed her glass down before pacing to the nearby windows to close the blinds. "Are you sure we're safe here?"

"Fort Knox," he reiterated.

She wished she had a tenth of his confidence.

Now suddenly more exhausted than she ever remembered being, she crossed back into the great room and stood with her back to the fireplace.

"What would you like the sleeping arrangements to be?"

How could she not have thought of that?

"I can be a gentleman and stay down here on the couch."

Or you can sleep upstairs... With me.

"Whatever makes you most comfortable."

Would she be able to fall asleep if he was next to her? On the other hand, would her fears cause her to toss and turn if he was in a different part of the house?

"And even if I share your bed, I can still be a gentleman."

Is that what she wanted? After all, he was still the man she'd surrendered herself to earlier in the evening. "I think I'll be able to rest better if you're closer to me."

"So will I."

"Do you mean that?"

"Oh yeah. I have a personal interest in your wellbeing."

"Thank you for saying that."

"Do we need to do anything for this lot?" He indicated the dogs who were curled up on various pieces of furniture. Bella had stretched out in front of the fireplace without Morgan noticing.

"I'll put them to bed." Or at least she'd try. She'd never actually done so before. "They've been known to get into mischief if they're free to roam the house at night."

"I can only imagine. Who's the instigator?"

"Well, right now Bella—the puppy—chews anything in sight. So watch out for your shoes. But generally it's Farrah. Because she's usually so quiet that her behavior is unexpected. Then there's Fifi." She looked with wide doe-eyes. "Even when she is naughty, she will act so loving that she escapes a scolding."

"Here's the million-dollar question... How do you tell them apart? They look identical."

"Different personalities, and Mom color coordinates their collars and leashes and ribbons. Walter—the alpha—is always in blue. If you can get him to do what you want, the others pretty well fall in line."

"Everyone follows the man who's in charge?"

"Oh sure. In real life too."

They exchanged quick grins, and she appreciated him for getting her mind off other, more distressing things.

She walked toward the crates, and a couple of the dogs looked at her. "Walter! Good night."

After yawning and stretching, he padded toward her.

As predicted, others followed suit. Bella tore across the space and ended up skidding partway on her bottom, making Morgan laugh.

Fifi paused to give Kane a great big slurping kiss on his forearm. "You two got acquainted outside."

"I remember her well." He gave her another patient scratch behind her ear.

After that, she pranced to her kennel.

"That was painless."

"The first thing that's gone smoothly all night."

Kane switched off the fireplace, then carried their glasses to the kitchen. She took a second to load their stemware into the dishwasher, then watched as he extracted his gun from inside his jacket. Was that really necessary? And if it was, maybe it was a good thing he'd have it close by. Still, the sight of the cold metal discombobulated her.

"Anything else we need to do?" he asked as he tucked the weapon behind him in the waistband of his jeans.

"That's it." Morgan debated turning off the lights but opted against it. If she had to get up unexpectedly, she didn't want to be searching for the switches.

Upstairs, she found extra toothbrushes and toiletries in the guest bathroom.

"Mind if I take a shower?"

"Feel free. I'd like you to be comfortable."

"You don't have to leave."

She wasn't sure she could survive seeing his naked body. "That's okay. I'll, ah…" She was going to say, "get ready for bed," but she had no idea what to wear. She had no pajamas

SIERRA CARTWRIGHT

here, and naked wasn't a consideration. Bra and panties, maybe?

Kane stripped off his shirt, then tossed it to her with a grin. "I know how much preserving your modesty matters to you."

Did he think of everything? "Thank you." Not that he hadn't already seen her bare butt.

She hurried to the bedroom and wiggled out of her dress, then unhooked her bra. The panties could remain in place.

With a towel wrapped around his waist, smelling of spring and spice from soap and mint from the toothpaste, he rejoined her. A droplet of water dripped from dark hair and traced a path down his forehead.

As she'd guessed, he was lean, muscled, and blessed with chiseled six-pack abs.

He couldn't be any sexier. Maybe they shouldn't stay in the same room.

"Which side is mine?"

With every other man, she'd had to accommodate his wishes. Having the option was a nice, novel experience. Generally she liked to be near the door, but not right now. Just in case. "That one." She pointed to the left. Then, holding on to the bottom of his T-shirt, she hurried to the bathroom and slammed the door closed, ignoring the soft chuckle that followed her.

When she returned, after stalling as long as she could, he was sitting up in the bed, a pillow propped behind him, his gun and wallet on the nightstand. His jeans hung from a bedpost, mere inches away. And thoughtfully, he'd switched on the lamp next to her side and turned down the bedcovers.

"I..." Her mouth was suddenly too dry to speak. And she forgot what she was going to say. To cover her awkwardness, she turned to close the door and secure the lock.

"Checked in with the team. All is peaceful and quiet."

"Thank you." She was grateful for his reassurance and that she hadn't had to ask.

She slid in beside him, and he turned onto his side.

"Let's get this over with." He dragged her against him and wrapped her in the comfort of his arms.

Breath whooshed out of her at his unexpected and shockingly bold move.

"Our bodies were going to end up touching, and I'm not having you staying rigid and not relaxing for half of the night."

His breath was warm on her skin, and the heat of his strong body comforted her.

"Relax, sweetheart."

How could she with his hard cock pressing into her?

Exhaustion claimed her, dragging her under, even though she was sure it wouldn't.

But sometime later, she drifted back into consciousness, realizing how completely entangled their bodies were. As she shifted, his manhood responded, pressing against her once more.

"You okay, sweetheart?"

His voice was impossibly husky, like it had been at the club.

As he stroked her arm, arousal unfurled through her in a gentle, insistent way. "Will you make love to me?"

"Morgan—"

"Please? I know my own mind. And I want it. Want you…"

"I have no expectations—"

"Tell me you have a condom with you, secret agent man."

CHAPTER FIVE

HAWKEYE

larm bells blared in Kane. Every instinct warned him he shouldn't continue.

Emotional landmines lay at every turn.

He'd cautioned her—how many times?—that he sucked at relationships. Ever since his messy divorce, he'd ruthlessly separated sex—fucking—from attachment. He'd been one hundred percent successful, until Morgan sashayed into his life.

When he'd danced with her at the wedding, then kissed her even though he shouldn't have, her responses had been honest. Vulnerability had radiated from her trusting, golden-colored eyes.

He'd had to shut down her attraction to him, not just for her sake, but for his own. One relationship that had crashed and burned into a blazing, costly dumpster fire had been enough to last him a lifetime.

Even though a tear had traced down her cheek, making him feel like shit, he'd reassured himself that he'd done the right thing by walking away.

Still, he'd never forgotten her, making him wonder how successful he'd been.

When he'd caught a glimpse of her at the Reserve, his cock rose at the way her long, brunette hair flirted with her shoulders. Her black dress barely covered feminine secrets he wanted to uncover.

He reminded himself she wasn't his. And that left her free to scene with anyone she wanted, make as many mistakes as she wanted to.

He could walk away before she noticed him.

But the truth hit him with a power he never expected.

There was no chance of him turning his back on the alluring beauty a second time.

Before he acted, the ridiculous, wannabe Dom—Lars—intruded, puffed himself up, and went in for the kill.

For a moment, Kane folded his arms and watched, debating his course of action. Of course he wouldn't let her play with someone so obviously unskilled. If anyone's hands were going to be on her body, making her writhe, they would be his.

She'd wanted him once. And he was arrogant enough to believe she'd choose his charms over the other man's.

But then Lars hadn't taken her very polite *no* for an answer and instead behaved with a level of aggression that pissed Kane off. And he'd had no choice but to act on it.

If he studied her hard enough, long enough, every one of her private thoughts was revealed—just to him. He'd rebuffed her once. So why was he sticking his nose in her business now?

He had an answer, but it wasn't the easy one.

She already knew he despised disrespectful assholes. But this was about her, which made it personal. If Soren had ejected Kane from the club, it would have been with her slung over his shoulder. Even with his ex, he'd never experienced this unholy, possessive air. Even though that might put him squarely in the asshole category as well, he wasn't capable of walking away.

Now she looked at him questioningly. "I mean, I saw all the stuff Logan had in his jacket. Seems Hawkeye operatives are prepared for anything. So you have to have condoms."

Kane shook his head to bring himself back to the moment. "Yeah. I do." But if the rest of the night went where she wanted it to, he might not have enough.

"Well...?"

"I've fantasized about making love with you."

She blinked.

"If that's what you want."

"Do I need to repeat myself? You're taking consent too far."

"No such thing, especially after the events of the day." He needed her to know she had full control, and even more, that she could change her mind whenever she wanted.

"It started before that. At the Reserve, and the spanking you gave me..."

He'd been hard the whole time. Her tight, curved derriere was more inviting than he'd even imagined.

"I think I'll sleep better, after the adrenaline and everything."

Kane shot her a quick grin. "Sweetheart, if we start this, you aren't getting to sleep anytime soon."

"Is that a yes?"

Fuck. Her voice had a tremulous, doubtful note that he hated. "I'm not going to rush through it. This will be on my terms as much as yours."

"Always a Dominant?"

"A Dom?" He shrugged. "Your Dominant? Yes."

"Then get on with the bossing and…"

"And?" Waiting, he tried to suppress his grin.

"And shit."

"Brave little submissive. Telling me what to do." He traced her lower lip. "I'll have you screaming my name and wrapped around me in under five minutes."

"Is that a challenge? Or a promise?"

God he loved her sass. "A guarantee. Want to set a timer?"

Her lips parted, and even though she didn't answer, he read the acknowledgment of the truth in her eyes. His possessive words turned her on. "Say it. Tell me I'm your Dominant."

She pursed her lips together.

"Your eyes don't lie."

Momentarily she squeezed her eyes shut. Then she looked at him. "Yes…"

With patience cultivated from years of strategic thinking, he waited.

"Yes, Sir."

"We understand one another." He moved between her legs, and she lifted her hips to greet him.

In seconds, he could ensure she was slick for him, sweep aside the gusset of her panties, and be inside her. But that wasn't what he was interested in yet. "I want the kiss we should have had two years ago."

"You're not going to…"

"Oh yes. I am. But first, this…" He brushed his lips across hers.

With a breathless moan, she wrapped her arms around his neck. She seemed to have no objections to skipping foreplay.

What kind of selfish lovers had she been with in the past?

Since the question annoyed the fuck out of him, he shoved it aside, vowing instead to show her a different path.

He untangled her arms and pinned them above her head.

Her breaths came faster and closer together. "You're getting it." Seeking the sweetness of her tongue, he kissed her again.

At first, as if uncertain, she was tentative. Then, as she responded, he required more, relentlessly tasting, taking.

When he lifted his head to look at her and grant a momentary respite, she didn't move. "You're going to open your mouth for me. Don't you dare hold back. Your days of being a good little girl are over."

Her eyes were hazy as if she were swimming in a mental fog.

"Am I clear?"

"You are, Sir."

"Then do as I say."

With a nod, she parted her lips.

Not enough. "Wider."

She curled her fingertips into her palms.

"That's better."

With purposeful intent, he lowered his head and claimed her mouth, tongue-fucking her hard, so deep that she couldn't be confused about what the motion simulated or how determined he was to be in control...thrust and parry, their tongues circling, dancing in prelude to a ritual as old as time.

Relentlessly he went on until all tension drained from her, and every part of her body relaxed. She wanted to forget the day's events? He'd ensure she did and had plenty of pleasurable things to think about instead.

She was right about sex being a sleep aid. In his experience, it was the most powerful elixir on the planet. Masturbation didn't even come close.

He didn't end the kiss until she was writhing, seeking his cock, struggling to pull her hands out of his grip. To wrap them around him, no doubt. Though he hadn't looked at a clock, it had definitely been less than five minutes.

His little submissive was even more eager than he'd hoped. So, so perfect.

Finally he relented and used his thumbpad to soothe her swollen lips.

"I've never been…"

"Get used to it." Now that he'd had a taste, he was addicted.

He released her wrists, then rubbed the skin in case his grip had been too harsh. Then he continued down her arms, then finally massaged her shoulders. "Now it's time to quit hiding from me."

"As if you'd let me."

He rolled over onto his side and propped his head on his upturned elbow. "I'd like you to stand over there." He pointed to a spot on the floor illuminated by the soft glow of the lamp. Cognizant of her nervousness, he'd be less than an arm's reach away. "Once you're there, you're going to remove the T-shirt to show me your breasts." She had no idea what he was going to ask of her. "Then when I say, you'll slip off your panties."

"It would be faster if I just took off everything right now."

"Not interested in fast, Golden Eyes."

She huffed. "I was afraid of that."

"Get on with it." He laced his voice with command making the words almost a growl.

Gentleman that he was, he sat up, then offered his hand to her. It was more than courtesy; it was a way to let her know he meant what he said.

Her grip a little uncertain, she accepted. Dawdling, she moved to the spot he'd indicated.

"That's it." He swept his gaze over her. Her hair was

charmingly rumpled. He hoped to make it a complete disaster. "The shirt?" he prompted. Once she returned it, it would be a long fucking time before he washed it. Instead he'd tuck it into his deployment bag and carry it with him when he was in the field. Anytime he wanted, he'd be able to breathe in her scent, that of sweet vanilla and tempting innocence. "You're stalling."

She finally complied, pulling the garment up and over her head, stretching high which lifted up her firm, full breasts.

Her beautiful areolas were a tantalizing dusky rose, and her nipples were tight swollen peaks. "Gorgeous breasts, Morgan."

She dropped the T-shirt onto the bedspread, then lowered her arms to her sides.

Kane was tempted to instruct her to lower her gaze and place her hands behind her neck. But there was plenty of time for submissive instruction later. Right now, he wanted to enjoy her shock at his orders. "Cup them and lift them up. Show them to me as if you'd like me to taste them."

She gasped.

"That wasn't a suggestion."

With a short nod, she complied.

"Do you play with them often?"

A faint red blush painted her cheeks. How was it possible for her to still be so shockable?

"No." She cleared her throat. "No, Sir."

"You never squeeze your nipples? Toy with them while you're masturbating?"

She glanced at the floor. "Once in a while."

"How about when you're with a partner?"

"Definitely not then."

"Because you don't want to offend or hurt his feelings?"

"Something like that."

"At the Reserve, you surely learned about power exchange and that you need to ask for what you need. I want to be clear that I expect you to speak up. My goal is to give you pleasure. If there's something you want more of or less of, I insist you communicate that. Don't hide from me." Kane's voice didn't allow for negotiation.

"I'll try."

"Let's start now. Play with your nipples in any way you prefer. Demonstrate what you like."

"This makes me feel so exposed," she admitted.

"Do you want to get out of your own way? If so, reframe your thinking. You're doing what I asked, pleasing your Dominant. You're safe with me. The freer you are, the more we'll both enjoy the experience."

Gently she drew her breasts together then brushed the tips of her nipples. They tightened into harder buds.

"You enjoy a gentle touch?"

"Since my nipples are so sensitive, yes. In class, some people talked about how much they liked clamps, and I'd die if a pair were affixed to me."

"Good to know. We'll add that to your limits list." Cock throbbing, he watched for a couple more minutes. She released a few gentle moans and began to undulate. If he didn't put a stop to this, he'd be inside her in under sixty seconds. "Good. Now stop."

She needed a few seconds to obey—long, tortuous moments that he wasn't sure he'd survive. Finally she complied. "Please place your hands behind your neck. It will display your body in a way I prefer."

"You don't ask for much."

"Golden Eyes, I've barely begun."

"I was afraid of that."

She'd gone to the club to be topped, and he was happy to be the man to do so. "Shoulders and elbows back a little more—opening up your chest." When she did, she arched her back slightly. "That's it."

Morgan kept her gaze trained on him, seeking approval.

"You're perfect."

Goose bumps trailed across her skin, but since the heater was currently running, he doubted she was cold.

"Remaining as you are, turn your back to me, then remove your panties and spread your legs."

Her pivot was somewhat sluggish. He'd never been with a woman completely new to BDSM. To have the opportunity to shape her reactions the way he wanted was heady indeed. "Naked for me, Morgan."

She took several seconds to work the material over her hips, then down her thighs.

Though he'd seen her ass at the club, her top had been covered, and he'd missed the twin dimples at the base of her spine. Adorable.

Her body formed a perfect hourglass shape, and he looked forward to closing his hands around her waist. "You've got a body made for fucking."

She tightened her buttocks.

"And a rear for spanking." Which suddenly he was compelled to do. "Shall I show you?"

"Yes," she whispered.

The answer he'd hoped for. "Then spread your legs as far apart as you can. Are you able to grasp your ankles?"

"I think so."

"Do your best. You can place your hands on your calves or knees if needed."

As she bent, her hair brushed the floor. She was limber enough to do as he asked. The view was enticing, so much so that he might require she do this every day. Maybe multiple times.

Kane stood and took the couple of steps that brought him

to her. Then he traced his fingertips up the backs of her thighs. His turgid cock demanded that he slide into her welcome heat. But he'd asked restraint from her, which meant he had to show it as well.

Concentrating on her, he teased her clit, making her jerk forward and let go of her ankles.

Frantically she pressed her hands to the floor to keep her balance. "That was unexpected, Sir."

"You're forgiven."

"But you're the one who—"

"You're not blaming me for the fact you're a disobedient sub, are you?"

She exhaled an annoyed huff. "No, Sir."

"I didn't think so. Back into position please." He gave her immediate attention when her sex was once again available to him. "When I take you, you will be totally ready for me.

"I think you'll find I already am."

"Is that an invitation?"

"Yes."

He teased her womanhood, then slid a finger inside her. "You *are* wet."

She shifted her weight, silently pressing backward.

Already she was more comfortable than she'd been even twenty minutes ago. He drew some of her dampness to her clit and made small circles there until she helplessly jerked against his hand. No doubt she'd come in thirty seconds, maybe less, if he kept it up.

Taking a step back, he licked his fingers dry.

"Sir?"

"Don't worry, sweetheart. You'll get everything you're asking for. Lift up for a moment." He slid a hand beneath her to hold her in place before adjusting his stance. Then he warmed up her skin to receive the slow, stinging slaps that he rained down on her ass cheeks and sit spot.

Tomorrow she might be a little uncomfortable, which would be fine with him. Watching her shift in her seat would be a joy unto itself. "Have you ever been taken from behind while standing up?"

"No."

He released her, but this time he didn't soothe away the hurt from his swats. "Are you willing to try?"

"Anything as long as I can have you inside me."

He didn't deserve someone as innocently trusting as she was. "Relax for a second. Stretch out. When you're ready, place your palms on the nightstand."

While she did that, he stripped off his underwear and grabbed a condom from his wallet. After rolling it down his length, he parted her labia, and used some of her own dampness to slide through her feminine folds.

She swayed and arched her back.

After ensuring she was ready, he captured her hips and pressed his cockhead to her entrance.

Gently she cried out. "Damn. You're big, Sir!"

"You can take me." He lifted her slightly onto the balls of her feet and bent his knees more. Then he reached between them to caress one of her nipples.

She purred. *"Ohh that's nice."*

Most definitely, she was sensitive.

He took her with the gentleness she deserved, easing himself in, pulling out to let her rest before sliding in again.

When he was fully seated, her muscles tensed. "You're there." He skimmed his fingers down her back, then over her belly, and finally lower to find her clit. "I've got you."

As he spoke, she allowed her head to fall forward, and her hair framed her face.

"Oh, Sir. Fuck me?"

A million times. And a million times more.

He moved in her, and she cried out.

They synched to one another as if they were meant to be, and he fucked her hard, bringing her to a screaming climax.

She clenched down on him. Morgan was hot and tight. *Mine.* He gritted his back teeth and eased his demanding cock from inside her.

"Sir?" She stood and turned, sweeping strands of her hair back as she looked at him. Her bottom lip was swollen, as if she'd been biting down on it as they fucked. "You didn't come."

"Oh, I am nowhere close to being done with you, sweetheart." And his cock would explode if he didn't find his release soon.

In a single move, he swept her up and placed her on the mattress.

With a smile, she parted her legs for him.

He kissed her again, stroked her nipples, then laved each of them before licking her pussy.

"Oh God. What are you doing to me?"

"Making sure you're ready so I don't hurt you." After all, now that he'd started making love to her, he didn't plan to ever stop.

"You're an amazing lover."

Her words snapped his remaining restraint. He plunged into her, claiming her in a way she was sure to understand.

He dragged her arms above her head again, trapping them. Instead of protesting, she grinned.

Everything about her was perfect for him.

He filled her again and again, giving as much as he could, making it about her.

"My God." Her eyelids fluttered. "I can't—I mean...I'm ready..." Her words jumbled together.

Now if he could only make her forget her own name. "Come for me."

After she did, crying out, he continued, this time making

sweet love to her, communicating things he didn't have words for...that he was here for her, every step of the way, that he'd protect and care for her. Kane had never made those silent vows to anyone else.

After brushing back her hair, he kissed her deeply before allowing his own climax.

Finally, both of them spent, replete, he lay on his side next to her, where he could read her expression.

She stroked his cheek. "I needed that. Thank you."

He kissed the top of her head before leaving her momentarily to dispose of the condom and to gather a warm washcloth.

When he returned she was asleep. So trusting and perfect.

He disturbed her long enough to bathe her pussy. Though she murmured a protest, she never woke up.

Rest, however, eluded him. Having sex with her complicated things as he'd always known it would. A taste had left him hungry for more, just like it had at the wedding.

What the hell was he going to do about the problem that was Morgan Holden?

Throughout the night as he checked on her, he was no closer to an answer.

Restless, sometime before dawn, he pulled on his pants and the shirt that smelled like her and headed downstairs.

The dogs stirred, taking an interest in what he was doing, but they didn't bark.

Using the code Morgan had given him, he unset the alarm, then headed outside into the crisp air to talk to the operatives who'd recently come on duty. Everything was quiet, and nothing had happened overnight.

One of the agents, Barstow, the leader for this particular team, handed over the bag containing the picture of the five dogs that they'd removed from the house last night.

Quick work. *Even for Hawkeye.*

"Inamorata needs you to call her."

Nodding, he moved away.

She answered right away. As usual, she dispensed with a greeting. "We've got a problem."

"Roger that."

"There was writing on the back of the photograph." She paused, which conveyed the seriousness of her information. "Could be a hit list."

"The hell?"

"Ms. Holden's name is on it."

Tension uncoiled in his stomach and reached every nerve ending. "Jesus."

"Powell has been notified and has opted not to inform Agent Holden or his sister."

Motherfucker. That didn't sit easy with him. Keeping secrets and telling lies never ended well.

"Last night you seemed overly concerned for her wellbeing." Inamorata's voice was laced with warning.

He barely managed to bite back a curse. "Need I remind you you're the one who suggested I stick with her when I informed you of the break-in at her parents' house?"

Though Kane repeatedly warned Morgan he was shit at relationships, neither of them had realized how deep this would go. "I'll do my job." No damn way was he walking away and trusting someone to take care of her. He was the best. No arrogance, just fact. And no one else had as much at stake.

"Do you need to be reassigned?"

"Try it." He'd never gone renegade. But he'd never had anyone matter like Morgan.

"So it *is* personal."

His spine went rigid. "You asking if I'll refuse to follow orders?"

"Mission first, Patterson." This time, there was no doubting her warning.

"This conversation is over." That was the politest way he could think of to tell a superior to stay the fuck out of his business.

"You'll be informed if anything changes."

With that, the line went dead.

Jesus H. He fought off the instinct to spike the goddamn phone into the patio.

In all his years in the military and working for Hawkeye, nothing had hit him this hard.

He shoved his phone into his back pocket.

Then he sought out a place where he wasn't giving an operative a clear line of sight, tipped the photo out of the bag, and used his thumbnails to flick back the prongs keeping the picture in place. He might not be able to keep all his fingerprints off it, but he'd do his best. At this point, now that Hawkeye had lifted evidence, did it even matter?

Once the frame was apart, Kane stared at the back of the picture.

No doubt it was a hit list, beginning with Harold Loughton and continuing with a list of the dog's names, beginning with Walter and ending with Bella. Then names of the family members: Gerard Holden, Pierce, Morgan, Laurel, and two he didn't recognize.

Hell and back.

The moment he was done putting the snapshot back in place, his phone rang.

Powell.

"So you know?"

Kane glanced around. "Surveillance team notified you?"

"You'd have had to have been inside the house to have any hope of Agent Barstow missing that."

Figured. In a way it gave him a measure of peace.

"And in that case, Ms. Holden might have seen you. Probably better that it was me."

"What are you doing about Pierce?"

"Same thing you're going to do about his sister. Keep it quiet until we have a good reason not to. He's at Aiken. Back country."

"And Morgan's safe with me."

"Keep your head on," Powell cautioned.

"Inamorata said the same. Want me to repeat what I told her?"

Powell laughed. "I think I can imagine. Team meeting at three p.m., if you want to remote in. Otherwise I'll send over an update."

"Copy that."

Resolved, he went back inside and placed the photo on the island. This may have been the crappiest mission he'd been on—and he'd had plenty that sucked.

But he had a job to do. Mission first. Which meant he couldn't let Morgan suspect a damn thing.

He sought out coffee and found a pound of premium stuff and figured out how to turn on the fancy brewer. He rarely used one that had more than a single ON/OFF switch.

"Kane?" Morgan asked, her voice sounding meek.

Damn. He turned to see her nearby, wearing her dress and flats. Her hair was still a sexy mess, and her smile was soft but hesitant, as if wondering what had changed between them.

The inevitable morning after nerves?

"Hey…" Kane smiled in return. "You look radiant." He beckoned her, and when she came to him, he folded her in his arms and kissed her. ·

She exhaled as if she'd needed the connection. Truthfully he appreciated it as well. "I thought you'd sleep in."

"The dogs need to go out."

Of course they did. He should have thought of that. Though he was an expert in munitions, he had no clue when it came to taking care of things with four paws. "Tell me what needs to be done."

"Thank you, but I'd never ask you to take care of that motley crew."

There was no fucking way he was allowing her outside in that getup, potentially bending over while surveillance equipment was trained on her. "I'm dressed for it."

She shrugged her agreement.

"You stay here, have some coffee."

"Hardly seems fair."

"After last night, you've earned a little break." Kane glanced at her with a seductive smile.

She blushed. "I can't believe we did that."

"Or that I'm ready to spank and fuck you all over again." After looking at her from head to toe, he gave her a piece of advice. "Rest up while you can. Pretty soon you won't be able to sit."

"I'm not sure I can now."

He grinned again.

"I'll, er, just let them out of the crates."

Lecherously he watched her, tracking the soft sway of her hips.

Once Walter was free, he headed to the back door. One by one, the others followed. The littlest one didn't quite make it as far as the door.

"I'll take care of that, then call the cleaning crew." Morgan sighed.

"What about the backyard once they're done doing what it is that animals do?"

"Mom has a daily service that takes care of the little details that go along with having five pets."

"Say no more." At the door, he disarmed the security system.

"Are the agents still there?"

"Next shift is on duty."

"Did you get a sitrep?

"Quick study." He grinned. "Those true-crime podcasts a good training ground for you?"

"It's a little more interesting when it doesn't affect my life."

And he wanted to be on the inside looking out. "In answer to your question, everything's quiet. And…" He pointed to the counter. "Inamorata sent this back."

"That's impressive."

Walter barked.

"We're approaching the all-hell breaking loose time of the morning."

"Got it." After donning his jacket, he opened the door and was almost swept off his feet by the explosion of fluff and excitement. "You gotta be tough to deal with this bunch."

"Not for the faint of heart."

Now that he was outside, he had no clue what to do. Just…watch them?

One of them, wearing a pink collar, dashed over and dropped a toy at his feet. "Thank you." Was he really talking to something that couldn't answer?

She tried again, this time dropping it on his foot.

Understanding dawned, and he prayed the other Hawkeye agents weren't laughing their asses off at him.

All the dogs were suddenly interested in the game of fetch, except Bella who mostly sat on her haunches and watched.

When they seemed to have depleted their energy, he opened the back door and they all dashed inside.

Morgan had prepared five dishes of food, refilled the water bowl, and poured two cups of coffee. Since the bag was gone from the counter, no doubt she'd also put the photo back in her parents' room.

She brought him a mug. "Black, I'm guessing. As long as it has caffeine, it will work. Eat when you can. Sleep when you can. And drink whatever passes for coffee?"

He accepted the offering and toasted her with it. "You get used to cream or sugar, you cry like a baby when it's not available."

"Better to suffer all the time then?"

"Better? No. Easier? Yes."

"Another interesting life philosophy." She took a seat at the table. "I texted my mom, but I haven't heard back. So I have no idea whether she's coming home or not."

"And the dogs?" He glanced at the pups who were snoozing in various patches of sunshine.

"I can't take them to the vet. I love them too much. I'm sure Mom is counting on that."

He took a seat across from her. "You've got a good heart." No doubt her mother and father weren't the only ones to take advantage of that fact.

"How could you not love this adorable pack?"

Fifi—if he had the name right—padded over to place her head on his lap, while Bella jumped up onto Morgan's. "What do we need to do today?"

"Since it's Sunday, I don't typically go to the office, but I do need some clothing and makeup if I'm staying here."

"What time do you want to go?"

Her eyes widened. "I forgot all about my car. At some point, we'll have to go to the Reserve, or I'll need to find a ride and hope it hasn't been towed away."

"It's at your house."

"How?" She scowled. "Never mind. Inamorata."

He lifted one shoulder. "She's good."

"But she wouldn't have known to do that except for you. I appreciate the way you're always looking out for me." She placed Bella back on the floor, walked over to him, then gently nudged Fifi aside before sliding onto his lap to straddle him.

"As I said, I have no expectations." But fucking damnation, his cock was already hard. "Morgan... Sweetheart."

She slid herself back and forth against his crotch. "I'd say regular cowgirl is about every bit as good as reverse cowgirl, Agent Patterson. Or is it Commander?"

"You're playing with fire, Golden Eyes."

"Is being burned all bad?"

There was a teasing, confident note in her voice that had been missing before now. And it was hot as fuck.

She scooted back a bit to unfasten the button at his waist and lower the zipper.

In that moment, he growled, lifting her off him so he could extract his wallet to pull out a condom before working his jeans down his legs.

He sheathed himself before stripping off her dress. *Holy hell.* "No bra or panties?"

Her smile held a touch of devilment. "I was hoping to have my wicked way with you, Sir."

Jesus. He'd thought she was perfect. Now she'd proven it. In daylight, he drank in her gorgeous body. "Last night, you looked beautiful. Now, in the sunshine, you're radiant." He lightly squeezed one of her breasts. "You can have your wicked way with me. But I'll have mine with you first." He sucked on the nipple, laving it until her whimper became a plea of need. "Lean back. Play with your pussy, show me when you're wet and ready for me."

All of a sudden, she hesitated.

"Do it."

Eyes wide, she nodded, grabbing one of his shoulders for stability.

Kane brushed a fingertip across her other nipple, bringing it to a firm peak. Then he captured two of her fingers. "Lick them. Make them wet."

Once she had, he lowered them to her pussy. After a few seconds, she seemed to lose her embarrassment and began to pleasure herself.

"That's it." He couldn't imagine anything hotter.

When she shook her head with wild abandon, he lifted her and set her on top of him, drawing her down in one long, forceful stroke.

Her toes pressing into the floor, she rode him as he thrust. With a ragged gasp, she reached for him again. Rather than letting her, he captured her hands behind her back. "You wanted to fuck me. Do it. Finish what you started."

She met his gaze. As always his words, his tone, made her eyes appear somewhat dazed. No other submissive had ever responded to him in quite this way. Then again, he'd never been this interested in anyone else before. Only Morgan triggered this deeply dominant urge.

"Oh!" Her lips parted, and her head fell backward.

"That's it." He placed his hands on her waist, lifting her, bringing her down, increasing their friction and the depth of his penetration.

Now that she'd matched his rhythm, he released one hand to press a finger against her clit.

Screaming, her internal muscles clamped down on him and she came, crying out his name.

When she blinked the world back into focus, he adjusted her position. "Lean on me and raise onto your toes."

Without hesitation, she did. And each time that she lifted herself, he spanked her ass, making her squirm on his cock.

"Sir!"

As their pace became more frantic, and he drew closer to an orgasm, he made his swats harder and harder.

She was gasping, lost in her pain and pleasure. "Sir!"

They came simultaneously, and then he held her close until they were breathing at the same place, replete and content.

When she pushed back from him, her hand splayed on his chest, she was wearing a triumphant smile. "Everything with you is new."

That stroked his ego in ways that should be illegal. "We've got a thousand more things to try."

"Oh?"

Now that she'd been the instigator and he hadn't turned her down, she seemed to have more confidence, and he was the direct beneficiary of that. "We both need sustenance and to gather our belongings."

"Duty calls?"

"More material from your podcast?"

"Trying to learn to speak fluent secret agent language."

"I'd say you're well on your way." He grinned. "If you want to clean up or shower, I'll make breakfast."

"Wait. You take care of the dogs, give me multiple orgasms when I didn't think that was possible, and you cook?"

"All that." He helped her to stand, and she smoothed her dress into place and picked up her cup. "Omelet okay for breakfast?"

"Oh yippee. Protein." She wrinkled her nose. "My favorite. Goes well with cold coffee."

"Maybe I can find a piece of bread or something for you. But you can't knock my omelet until you've tried it." He stood and pulled up his jeans, fastening and zipping them and sliding his wallet back into his pocket.

"A croissant or donut, maybe an éclair would be better. I need energy."

"We can send out for more provisions if needed."

"Or stop by a bakery? I doubt you'll find much more than the basics. Chef generally brings things with him."

"They have a chef?"

"As you saw last night, there's plenty of orange juice and champagne in there. Mom does enjoy her mimosas, but she's not big on real food. Dad goes to the office most days, and he doesn't come home until maybe nine or ten. So he fends for himself."

"Does the chef have a code to the alarm?"

"I…" She shook her head. "No idea. It never occurred to me."

"Shoot Inamorata a text with the name?"

"Yeah. I'll do that." She wrapped her arms around herself. "How many more things am I missing?"

"No one can remember everything. As things come to you, you can send them over."

"Yeah. Maybe I need one of those mimosas."

"Want me to make you one?"

"I wish." She sighed. "But no. I probably need a clear head. But I'll drink a bucketful when this is over."

"You'll deserve them." He grabbed both of their mugs, then dumped the contents. "Need a fresh cup?"

"I'd like one from a coffee shop."

"Let me guess? Sweet, drowning in whipped cream?"

"With chocolate." She made a back-and-forth motion with her hand. "Drizzled all over the top." Leaning against the counter while he pulled out a pan and cooking utensils, she crossed her legs at the ankle. "And I like to lick it off the top." She demonstrated what she meant.

He picked up a spatula and advanced on her. "Unless you want to be turned the other way, have your dress yanked up around your waist and feel this on your rear, I suggest you escape while you can."

"Uhm…" She looked at him, then the implement, then back at him again.

He waved it through the air, and it whistled threateningly. "Make your choice before I make the decision for you."

CHAPTER SIX

HAWKEYE

Less than an hour later, the dogs were snoozing in their crates, and she and Kane were heading to her home, via her favorite coffee shop that wasn't too far out of the way.

Morgan glanced across the vehicle's interior at Kane. "Are you sure you don't want anything?"

While the breakfast he'd made was tasty, a search of the refrigerator and freezer had yielded no carbs.

"More than positive. Thanks."

"I admire your restraint." As for her, she had none. "But you're not going to steal mine, right? Like no surreptitious drinks when you think I'm not paying attention. Or pretending you don't like sugar when secretly you do?"

"Sweetheart, your drink is as safe with me as you are."

She narrowed her gaze. "Is that supposed to be reassuring?"

He laughed, low and super sexy.

"The froufrou whatever is all yours, Golden Eyes."

If she continued to hang out with him, she was going to burn the calories. The way he looked at her sent shivers racing through her. How was it possible for her to still be this hungry for sex after everything they shared? No matter how many times they made love, her lust wasn't sated. The more she got, the more she wanted.

Because her mind was in sudden danger of spiraling into naughty territory, she refocused on the app on her phone, scrolling to the screen where she could modify her usual drink order. She opted to add an extra shot of espresso, additional whipped cream, and a double helping of chocolate drizzle.

Both happy and guilt-free, she confirmed the order.

Since his vehicle was so big, he couldn't fit the SUV into the small shack's parking lot. So he found a space nearby and turned off the engine, then hurried around to her side.

Instead of offering a hand, he closed his hands around her waist and lifted her from her seat. For several seconds, he held her in his firm grip, his cock pressing against her. It seemed she wasn't alone in her neediness.

Finally he placed her on the ground. "I can go in by myself, you know."

"I'm sure you can. But I'm not going to let you."

After closing her door, he reached for her hand.

"Are you carrying this protector thing too far?"

"No." He shook his head. "This has nothing to do with that."

"Ah. Being gentlemanly?"

"Still wrong. I like touching you."

Inside the store, he stood on duty near the entrance, his arms folded across his chest. Even his jacket couldn't hide all his sexy, rippling muscles.

After dropping a bill in the tip jar, she headed to the counter where she picked up her coffee and removed the lid to ensure the drink was correct. Then she turned to face Kane and found his gaze was trained on her.

Suddenly an impish, irresistible urge came over her, and she licked the whipped cream, making sure to exaggerate her motions and touch her upper lip with her tongue.

He dropped his arms to his sides.

Taking it as a warning, she recapped her beverage and hurried over to him. "It's exactly as I ordered it."

He glared at her. "Is it?"

"Exactly. Sir."

"How many times do you need to be warned?"

"The whole being burned thing? Is that what you're talking about? As I've said before, maybe it's not all that bad."

"Oh, sweetheart."

Several young adults entered, laughing and giggling.

Once they passed, he opened the door and nodded for her to precede him.

As she crossed the parking lot, she was hyperaware of his gaze on her rear. Still pushing her luck, she glanced over her shoulder. "Planning my next spanking?" Dear God, she hoped so.

They headed for her condominium complex, and she couldn't help but hazard a glance at him.

Their time together had been so surreal. And once they were back at her place, there really was no reason for them to stay together. She'd have her car, and if there was still surveillance at her parents' home, she would be completely safe. "Kane…"

Instantly he looked over.

"I'm realizing I've been a burden long enough."

"That's not a word I'd use to describe you."

She gave a half-hearted laugh.

He'd mentioned he was currently on a Denver-based assignment, and in the morning, they both had jobs they needed to get back to. "I wanted to say thank you."

"You're not getting rid of me that easy."

Her heart jumped.

"We'll take it one step at a time."

"But…" Truthfully she didn't want to say goodbye.

"I'm staying with you for the time being." He drummed his fingers on the steering wheel. "Save us both a lot of aggravation by not arguing." His voice held a note of finality.

Because that's what she wanted, she smiled and nodded.

They lapsed into silence, and she picked up her cup, needing to tip it back quite a bit to get some of the drink from beneath the outrageous toppings.

A few minutes later, he turned into the underground parking garage. The vehicle barely fit beneath the height-restriction bar. "This is unnerving."

With every turn, she was afraid the top would scrape on the concrete beams. "You're not even fazed. Nerves of steel?"

"At least I'm not worried about IEDs or grenades being lobbed at us."

And she'd spent the last few years getting through school and trying to establish a career. There was no possible way she could hope to understand a man as complex as Kane.

He backed into place, and when she opened her door, she realized that he was actually taking up two spots because the SUV was so wide.

With him half a step behind her, they headed to the bank of elevators where he pressed the call button and glanced around. "No access codes needed?"

"The building has a security guard, and there are cameras everywhere. So I feel safe."

He nodded. "Anyone can get in the parking garage and ride the elevator."

Unease traced through her. Of course he was right. But until last night, she'd felt perfectly safe, secure in the world. But now…?

"You have an alarm system for your place?"

"Uhm…"

"I'll have Hawkeye install one."

Sounded pricey. "How much does that cost?"

When he didn't respond, she tightened her grip on her cup. "Kane. I can't let you pay for something like that."

His jaw was set, resolute.

She exhaled her frustration. "Do you ever change your mind about something?"

"Not once it's made up. Especially when there's no doubt as to the correct course of action."

"But…" The doors slid open, and once they were sealed inside, she pressed the number for her floor and resumed her argument. "You are not responsible for me."

"Sweetheart?" With a lethal smile, he leaned toward her. "If you know what's good for you, *shut the fuck up.*"

Morgan brought her back teeth together. Confounding, annoying man.

After they exited the compartment, he followed her to her unit, and he took the key from her and didn't step back until he'd pushed the door open and glanced around.

When they were inside, his size and presence dominated her small condo.

He locked the door and swept his gaze over every single detail including the stack of mail and the glass she hadn't loaded into the dishwasher before leaving last night. A lifetime ago. "Make yourself comfortable while I grab a few things."

He nodded and crossed the room, nudging aside the blinds to look out the windows. Pierce behaved the same way, much to their father's annoyance. He'd snap at Pierce for playing his ridiculous secret agent games.

In her room, she grabbed a bag from her bedroom closet. After changing out of the previous night's fancy dress and tossing her discarded clothing into the laundry hamper, she pulled on fresh underwear, then dressed in a long-sleeve T-shirt, cozy jeans, and athletic shoes. At least now she'd be less self-conscious when she stepped outside at her parents' home where Hawkeye agents were observing her every move, whether she could see them or not.

Not knowing how long to pack for, she grabbed enough clothes for a few days, rationalizing she could come back here after work even if she were staying in Parker.

Then she went into the bathroom to grab cosmetics, a hairbrush, and some toiletries.

In shock, she froze in her bedroom doorway. Kane was in there, going through her bag.

"Do you have anything sexy?"

As if he had every right to be in here, he was totally unapologetic.

"What are you doing?"

"Making sure you thought of everything. Bottom drawer?" he guessed.

"I don't want to even know how you know that."

"It's those patterns I talk about. Everyone is different, but there are some generalities. Your top drawer is going to be for the things you wear most: bras, socks, panties. Then probably T-shirts, jeans, workout gear. And the items you wear the least will be in the bottom drawer." He paused.

Along with the vibrator she'd bought one evening when she'd gone shopping for a bachelorette party with Jennifer.

"For example, lingerie. Maybe some cash or jewelry you'd like to keep hidden." He shot her a seductive grin. "Or a few private belongings that you don't want nosy visitors to see."

Like you?

"So that's where I'll start."

There was no stopping him when he was on a mission.

Moments later, he pulled out a sexy piece that she'd never worn. The nightie had a V-neck that plunged almost to her belly button, and like the dress she'd worn to the club, the garment would barely cover her rear.

The steamy glance he sent her direction rocketed shivers of anticipation through her.

"This will work nicely." He tossed it to her. "Put it in the bag."

Instead of arguing, she did as he instructed, along with the other items she'd just gathered.

Instead of standing, Kane continued his search. "Wonder what else is in here?"

She squeezed her eyes shut. How was it possible for him to still embarrass her?

Naturally he pulled out the vibrator.

"It's like the one we saw at the club. The scene we watched."

Vividly she recalled every detail.

"Where the Top had his bottom in that secluded spot, and he was wringing orgasm after orgasm from her."

As if he was talking about what he intended to do to her, her pulse quickened.

"It'll suit my purposes."

He tossed it into her piece of luggage, then zipped it closed before picking it up. "Anything else?"

She grabbed her purse. "Let me just grab my work tote bag. It's in my office."

When she reached the room, she stopped in shock, staring at her desk. Her purse thumped to the floor.

"Morgan?" Kane called out. Seconds later he was at her side, studying her, glancing around the room.

This can't be happening.

"Talk to me."

"My computer… It's gone."

Will this nightmare ever end? Morgan paced in front of the fireplace in her parents' home. The dogs lazed around, content. And Kane sat on the couch, leaning forward, saying nothing as he studied her.

Even as he'd notified Hawkeye of the situation, he'd immediately hustled her from her condo and loaded her into his vehicle.

During the drive, he'd received several more calls, and he'd talked as she stared disbelievingly out the windshield.

He arranged for a sweep of her home, a tail to follow them, and even takeout that included plenty of sweets to go along with the protein. Of course they needed to eat, but that was the last thing on her mind.

When she'd asked if they needed to get clothing for him, he shook his head. Since he never knew when or if he'd make it home, he kept several changes of clothes in his vehicle.

When her phone chimed, she lunged for it. "It's my mom."

He nodded.

We land around midnight.

"They'll be home tonight."

"Good." He nodded. "That means we don't have to spend the night here."

"That's true. But... I guess..." Where would she go? Kane was right about her needing a security system, and she didn't want to drive home in the middle of the night. And sleeping there, knowing someone had walked in...

"What?"

"Maybe I can go to a hotel."

With lightning-fast reflexes, he was on his feet and across the room to capture her shoulders in a fierce grip. "Listen to me, Morgan, and don't make me repeat myself. I'm not leaving you alone. You're stuck with me."

"So what's your plan?"

"You're coming to my house. And, no, I'm not asking."

"When were you planning to tell me this."

"Need to know."

She set her chin. "More fancy lingo?" That she was familiar with. "You were going to tell me at the right place and time and not a minute before."

"You're dealing with a lot."

"And you didn't want to argue with me."

He grinned without mirth. "You're too smart to disagree with my professional assessment."

"There really is no end to your arrogance."

Very slightly, he loosened his grip. "Tell me where I'm wrong. Your private space was violated, and you were robbed. You're not going to want to stay there. And it turns out the security guard saw nothing. We're reviewing surveillance video, but…"

"Yeah." There was no need for him to finish. They both knew the tapes would reveal nothing.

"A hotel isn't safe. Too many entrances, people. Access to my place is easier to control. Quiet neighborhood. Large lot. Little traffic, and every approaching vehicle can be intercepted. Do you have a better option?"

"I wish I understood. Why would someone want my computer? I don't have anything that interesting on it." She sighed. "I suppose it can be used to access the server at work? But who cares about that?"

Something passed through his eyes, dark, maybe foreboding. "Do you know something you're not saying?"

He shook his head. "Thinking, like you are. Any more questions?"

That he'd have an answer for.

"What time do you want to leave? Now?"

"The dogs will need to go out, have dinner, be put to bed."

"I'll take them outside if you want to handle things in here, maybe unpack the food bags."

Just because she had no appetite, didn't mean he wasn't hungry.

Like a natural, he called for Walter.

The alpha of the pack cocked his head and then turned his wide eyes in her direction. "Outside," she told him.

He stood and pranced toward the backdoor wagging his tail, the rest of the dogs following along in a happy parade.

"You're a natural, Kane."

"They're a good bunch."

She nodded her agreement. Since they no longer had to spend the night, she went upstairs to grab her bag and be sure everything was back where it should be so that her mother didn't have a meltdown.

While they'd been out, the housekeepers had performed a between-service visit. They hadn't done a deep clean, but they'd swept and mopped the kitchen and sanitized kitchen counters, along with general tidying up.

The door to her parents' room was open, and she glanced inside.

The photo that she'd placed in there earlier was now upright—no doubt the cleaners had figured it was a mistake.

Morgan debated what to do. A message—potentially— had been sent by whomever had broken in. Shouldn't her parents realize that?

Maybe it would make them take what had happened more seriously?

With a sigh, a creepy sensation washing over her, she put it back where she found it.

"Everything okay?"

Screaming, she jumped. Her hand pressed to her heart, she turned to face Kane.

"Sorry. Didn't mean to startle you. Thought you heard me."

"No." She hated all this skullduggery. "The picture..."

Crossing to her, he draped his arm around her shoulder and walked her to the door. "Let's go."

"I'm ready." *More than.*

"Your bag?"

"I think that's the only thing I have up here."

Downstairs, she fed the dogs, then picked at her own meal.

"Wine?" he offered. "Still some left from last night."

"Do you have any at your house? Or we can take last night's with us. Maybe a couple of extra bottles. They'll never miss it, and their delivery date is coming up." She tipped her head back. "And no, I have no idea if the liquor store has the alarm code." How many people could come and go as they pleased? "Don't say it. I'll let Inamorata know."

He nodded. "Keep listening to your podcasts."

"I may be done."

"Oh?"

"I'm freaking myself out. Jumping at shadows, suspicious of everything."

"Things will return to normal eventually. Or a new version of it. This will be behind you and the fear will subside."

She nodded, drinking in his words. After all, his was the voice of experience. "I may take a break though, from the true-crime shows on television."

"Excellent plan."

Still, she held onto his comforting words as she got the dogs settled for the night, then turned off some of the lights.

Kane took out the trash—and no doubt checked in with the Hawkeye team—while she placed her bag near the door. Then she grabbed a couple bottles of wine and placed them in a travel tote she found in the pantry.

"Ready?" he asked when he came back inside.

In under two minutes, they were pulling out of the driveway, and she glanced in the sideview mirror, looking back at the house. "Is the Hawkeye team still there?"

"Inamorata's leaving them there for the time being."

That reassured her some. But it also meant surveillance would end at some point. "I probably need to update Pierce."

"Feel free to call him. My guess is Powell's been in touch."

"And he's more likely to get through?"

"Inamorata's got influence at HQ."

Probably in the farthest reaches of the universe as well.

As he'd guessed, she reached her brother's voicemail, so she settled for sending him a text. "Uhm, does he know I'll be at your place?"

"I'd bet on it."

"Do I have any secrets anymore?"

"Depends what you're talking about." He shot her a purposeful glance. "There's a whole lot of them I still want to uncover. Tonight, even."

"Your voice…"

Silently he waited for her to go on.

"It's…well…it chases other thoughts from my mind." Most likely that was his intention. He used tone and inflection so skillfully that he could alter her pulse rate.

His home was on the western outskirts of Denver, in an older, well-established neighborhood. Houses were on large lots, and some even had horses. "This is fabulous."

"Relaxation will be mandatory at my place."

When they arrived, he parked the monster SUV in the three-car garage, then helped her out and grabbed her bag and tote.

The door leading into the house was metal and thick enough that it could secure a bank vault.

On the wall, he lifted a plastic-looking flap and pressed his fingertip against a small pad. Instantly a beam of green light bounced from a tiny sensor resembling an eye.

Had they been sucked into a science-fiction movie?

Without her needing to ask, he explained. "Facial-recognition scanner."

Moments later, a keypad lit up.

"You have to go through all that before even entering a code?"

"State of the art. But nothing is perfect."

It was a whole lot better than anything she'd ever seen. "That's not what you're planning to install at my place is it?"

"No. Yours will analyze the shape of your breasts."

She gasped. "You would *not* do that."

"Maybe if it automatically sent a picture to my phone."

His face was set in such a serious line that she had no idea whether or not he was joking.

"In the morning, we'll program the system with your biometrics."

He glanced inside the well-lit space before indicating she could walk in. Immediately he followed her.

A soft chirp filled the room, then the sound of a woman's voice seemed to bounce off the walls. *"Welcome home, Agent Patterson."*

"Hello, Polly."

"Polly? Morgan asked.

"Whole house computer. But don't tell her that. She thinks she's the queen of the multiverse."

The moment he closed the door and placed her bag on the floor, another chirp filled the air. *"System armed."*

"Now I'm unsure whether I'm in Wonderland or an episode of the Jetsons."

"We have a guest, sir? Well, isn't this a delight? And so unusual."

He scowled. "Polly, say hello to Ms. Holden." He shrugged. "Unless she'd prefer to be called Morgan."

"Hello, Ms. Holden. Unless you'd prefer to be addressed as Morgan."

Delighted, she grinned. "Morgan is fine. Nice to…" She raised her eyebrows, a bit perplexed as to how to continue. "Meet you."

"Likewise. If you can remind him not to be an ass in the mornings, I think we can be friends."

Oh my God.

"Polly, I'm going to unplug you, do you understand?"

"Ms. Holden, I'm sure you can see what I was referencing."

She couldn't help but laugh.

Kane led the way to the kitchen, and as they approached, under-cabinet lights turned on, bathing the space with gentle light. "That happens automatically?"

"It's a nice feature, especially in the middle of the night." He placed the tote on a quartz counter and pulled out the wine. "Can I pour you a glass?"

Maybe she could drink straight from the bottle, save multiple trips to the refrigerator. "Please."

"Coffee delivery occurred this afternoon, so you won't be a cranky bastard tomorrow."

Wide-eyed, staring at his scowling features, she mouthed, "Cranky bastard?"

"The refrigerator and cupboards have been restocked."

"You sent the notification to my phone, Polly." He pulled out two glasses. "She's glitchy. Ignore her ramblings."

"I beg your pardon."

"Polly, give it a rest."

"I'm sure you'll let me know when you need me again, cranky bastard."

He poured the wine as Morgan laughed. "I've got to know more about Polly and her over-the-top personality."

"You can blame Bonds for that."

She blinked. "Like as in Julien Bonds? The tech genius billionaire? You *know* him?"

"We're not friends. But Hawkeye has a licensing agreement to use certain technology that's not widely available. As I mentioned, Polly is a whole-house computer."

"Ah-hem."

"I stand corrected. She's known as my chief of staff."

"Someone has to keep you organized."

She accepted the drink he offered. "I'm betting it's—she's? —expensive."

"I'm worth it."

"Polly…" He growled. "That's it. Leave the room and quit eavesdropping."

"This is an illustrated example of what I put up with, Ms. Holden."

"Morgan is fine." Was she really having a conversation with something she couldn't see?

"You've been warned, Polly."

A small red light in the corner of the living room winked out. Until it did, Morgan hadn't even been aware of its presence. "Is this banter normal?"

"I'd report her, but Bonds would laugh his ass off. The upgraded line seems to be, shall we say, imbued with his personality. It's my understanding that he actually writes the code."

"With the number of projects he's involved in"—from computers to phones to AI to holograms and more—"I can't believe he's got time for that." And she'd recently heard something about him going through a devastating loss.

"Now that you've met my chief of staff…" He waited for a moment—to ensure the computer wouldn't respond?— before nodding and continuing. "Come on in. Let me show you around so you can get settled."

His lair was sparse, comfortable but not fussy, with

several massive pieces of furniture grouped around a fireplace and a home-theater-size television. Other than the pillows that matched the couch and chair, there were no throw blankets or rugs on the floor. The two lamps on end tables were utilitarian rather than decorative.

"I went to a furniture store right after my divorce. Salesperson sold me everything I needed in under thirty minutes."

Which evidently included barstools for the kitchen island and a table with seating for four.

"Follow me. I'll show you around."

On this level, he had a study and a workout room with equipment she'd never seen. "You spent a little more time designing this."

"Hired a guy out of New Orleans who designs fitness centers for hotels and gyms."

When it came to his physique, he wasn't afraid to spend money. For good reason. Being lean and fit probably helped keep him alive.

Before they headed upstairs, he grabbed her bag. There was an enormous loft area that was empty, a guest bedroom, full bathroom, and then a ridiculous suite that was obviously his bedroom.

He placed her bag in one of the closets that had a built-in dresser. Her one item in the cavernous space looked ridiculous.

Then he showed her to her bathroom, with a soaker tub beneath a beautiful frosted-glass window. "I've never seen anything like this."

"The previous owners had it remodeled. The real estate agent promised me that ladies prefer it this way."

"They prefer having their own space?" She pressed a hand to her mouth in fake shock. "You mean rather than picking up their partner's towels or dirty clothes? And other…things."

He laughed. "I guess it was worth the extra money they wanted for it?"

"I'd say so."

"You're welcome to as many baths as you want."

"You may never see me again."

"Just keep the beverages coming?"

That sounded like heaven. "I suppose I could have Polly tell you if I run out?"

He rolled his eyes to the ceiling and placed a finger to his lips. "Don't wake her up. For the love of God, just don't."

She laughed. This was a side of him she hadn't seen, and she liked it. Everywhere else, he was on guard, hyperalert. But it seemed like he'd created a sanctuary here, a place where he could turn off the stress, or at least dial it back. "Is your bathroom as wonderful?"

"Only if you like luxury."

He had a steam shower and so many knobs that she had no idea how he even managed to get the water to turn on. "I think there are fewer options on a fighter jet."

"You could be right."

Here, like in the other room, there was a window, but his was clear, showing a view of the majestic nearby foothills. "Your home is lovely. I see why you chose it." Even beyond what he'd said about the amount of property and how secluded it was.

"My favorite feature is the hot tub."

"Really?"

"Highly recommend a soak. You up for it?"

She wrinkled her nose. "I'd love to, but I didn't bring a bathing suit."

"No clothing allowed."

"Are you…" She blinked. "You mean that, don't you?"

"Residue from laundry detergent plays havoc with the system."

"But you mentioned surveillance, right? There's Hawkeye people watching us."

He grinned. "I have robes, and I'll help protect your modesty. I also have a few trees that will obscure the view."

His offer was more than tempting. Sitting outside after being cooped up so much this weekend definitely appealed. "You talked me into it."

"You'll find towels in your bathroom closet. The robe will be hanging from a hook behind the door. When you're ready, I'll meet you downstairs."

She nodded.

When she was back in the spa-like space, she stripped and changed into the utterly wonderful but too-big, fluffy, white garment. She'd stayed at luxury hotels that weren't this fabulous. Maybe it was time to do some renovations at her place.

Then she sighed. Another reminder that, like he said, this horrible situation would end, and she'd return to her normal life. Not that she had any idea what that looked like anymore.

Fortunately she'd brought along some clips and bands so she could sweep her hair into a ponytail and secure her locks in place.

Morgan descended the staircase, lights illuminating the way as she went. More niceties she'd like to install in her condo. Though with the way things were adding up, she may have to take out a second mortgage to pay for them.

He was waiting for her, plastic cups in hand. Made sense since glass would be a bad choice outside.

French doors led to the backyard. "Polly, disarm."

The lock snicked.

"This seems like such a normal feature, I mean, knowing what you had to do to get inside when we arrived."

"It's not normal glass. And it can't be opened unless I've already complied with the system requirements."

"Complicated." *And necessary?*

Small torches provided enough lighting to see by but not so much that it ruined the ambiance.

"Hold this?"

She accepted his drink while he removed the heavy lid from the tub, and she took the opportunity to look around.

Near them, a wrought iron table with chairs occupied the center of a concrete slab. Huge planters framing the patio were empty. Because it was late in the season? Or had he never planted anything? As infrequently as he was home, the latter was the most likely explanation.

Solar lamps were everywhere, outlining paths, providing beauty as well as safety.

She turned back to see steam rising from the water. He pressed a button, and bubbles exploded in playful bursts from numerous nozzles. "Looks so inviting."

"Every time I'm headed back from an assignment, I look forward to this."

"I see why."

He dragged a chair closer to them, then, evidently not nearly as concerned about being watched as she was, he removed his robe and dropped it on the padded seat.

After climbing the couple of attached stairs, he sank into the water, extending a hand for the cups that he slid into built-in holders. "Your turn."

Pressing her lips together, she reached for the knot in her belt but hesitated, looking around. As he said, there were huge trees that offered some privacy. Neighbors weren't close, but operatives—and binoculars, maybe night-vision equipment—were. "How am I supposed to do this?"

"Dreaming of the day that you'll just drop it and come to me like the goddess you are."

She skeptically tipped her head to one side. "That's not happening."

"For now, lift up your hem and come down this step."

Until he pointed it out, she hadn't realized she could enter in stages.

"I'll stand with my back to you, and you can undress and dive beneath the surface if you want to."

"Am I being ridiculous?"

"Not at all."

But she was, and they both knew it, which made her appreciate his reassurance even more. She'd never been with someone this courteous and considerate.

Somehow she managed to get in without soaking the robe. And with the way he stood, and the landscaping obstructing sightlines, she felt comfortable. "You've really got a sanctuary here. I was trying to think of the right word. Fortress also comes to mind, but you have amenities that make it comfy."

"I hope that means you can relax?"

"You've made sure of that. Thank you." She accepted her cup of wine that he extended to her. Then she tipped her head back to look up. "I can't believe how clear it is." A few high clouds floated overhead. A partial moon hung from the inky darkness, and dozens of stars twinkled in the distance. "It seems like forever since I took the time to enjoy the night sky." She was so caught up in work, trying to impress her boss and her dad that she often worked late. In the evenings, she'd arrive home exhausted, flipping on the television, mindlessly letting it blare while she prepared a quick dinner and ate in front of one of her favorite shows. When was the last time she'd escaped to the mountains? They were so close, less than a forty-five-minute drive away, and she could be in a different place and time.

The fact her life had become so small was one of the reasons she forced herself to get out of the house. The meetings with the Carpe Diem Divas were a blessing. Occasionally she attempted to meet men. She'd recently attended a speed-dating event where she'd made no connection with anyone. That one and only attempt had been an abject failure, a waste of both money and time.

She brought her head forward to look at Kane and to take a drink of her wine. Soaking and sipping was decadent, easing away the day's worries. Here, it was as if they were in their own little world. Until this moment, rolling her shoulders, she hadn't realized how on edge she'd been. "So how is it that you get deliveries here, even stocking your refrigerator? I'm surprised you'd allow something like that."

A quick smile made his lips quirk. "Are you saying I'm paranoid?"

She made a circle over her head to indicate she was a perfect angel and would never infer anything like that.

"You'd be correct. The service I use is contracted by Hawkeye."

"Why am I not surprised?"

"So all of the people are vetted. And Polly streams video to my phone from the moment someone nears to the moment they pull away."

"Even from inside the house?"

"Even that. The premises can be locked down too. If someone gets in, it's not likely they'll get out before I arrive. Or if I'm away, someone from work."

"You called my parents' home Fort Knox, but this really is."

"Fewer people come and go here. And Hawkeye provides remote monitoring."

"You better not tell me they're going to watch us sleep." She shuddered. "That's just weird."

"I promise you…" He leaned forward. "Whatever I do to you in my bedroom is private. No one will hear your moans." Even in the dim lighting, she saw his eyes darken with desire. "Or cries."

She gulped. "That's…reassuring."

Suddenly the motor fell silent, and the bubbles stopped rising to the surface.

"Do you want me to turn the jets back on? Or do you want to enjoy the peace?"

The evening was quiet, so much so that she only heard the rustling sounds of nature. "This is idyllic."

"Agree. Would you like some more wine while we enjoy it?"

If he was as courteous with his former wife as he was with her, she had no idea how he was divorced. "Did you spoil your ex this way?"

"Maribeth."

She hadn't expected him to be so forthcoming. "From what I can see, you don't appear to be shit at relationships." Then a painful truth hit her. That wasn't what this was. And she needed to remember that fact. She was connected to a case he was working on and was employed by the same company that her brother was.

"To be fair, I don't blame her."

Intrigued, Morgan put down her empty cup.

"I'm gone a lot. And back then I was in the military. Special forces, and we spun up—deployed—a lot and often on a moment's notice."

Quietly she waited for him to go, wondering if he would.

"I missed most of her birthdays, all our anniversaries. Can't remember being home for Christmas. And Valentine's Day really bothered her. I should have at least figured out how to send flowers, candy. Something like that."

She winced. "That had to be tough. But surely as a military spouse, she had to expect that, right?"

"I wasn't special forces when we met, and there's a reason divorce rates are so high. Military is difficult enough, but I could be gone up to nine months of the year. Often slept less than five hours a day for weeks at a time. When I was home, I wasn't really there. Maybe physically but not mentally." His shrug was fatalistic. "When the person you love isn't around to provide affection or memories, it can be tempting to make them with someone else."

"Is that what happened?"

Unflinchingly he met her gaze. "I was in Africa when she sent me a picture of an ultrasound."

"She was pregnant?" Did he have a child she didn't know about?

"My first reaction was utter joy that I was having a child, becoming a father. And I sure as hell wanted to be a better one than my own dad. He was a cop. I have no idea how many affairs he had before my mom finally called it quits. So damn many arguments with him storming out of the house. But I'd have a chance to do things differently."

She held her questions, letting him set the pace.

"It wasn't mine."

The air was knocked out of her lungs, not only because of Maribeth's affair but the callousness of the way she'd informed Kane. "Oh, Kane."

"I swung through a gamut of reactions—disbelief to rage. Anger, then back again. Like I was on a roller coaster. About a week later, I called her, told her we could figure it out. That I forgave her, and we could raise the baby together." He laughed, a sardonic pain-filled sound. "Her response? Fuck you. She wasn't asking for my forgiveness. She wanted a divorce."

"And you really didn't have a choice?"

"Marriage takes the agreement of two people. Divorce only requires one."

"That's a horrible situation to be in."

"She wanted to stay married until after she had the baby.

Didn't want to lose my benefits. But when she went into labor, it was another man there with her."

Despite the warmth, she was chilled.

"I gave her everything she asked for. I figured she deserved it for putting up with me through the years. If I drove her to that, I was no better than my father."

He was every bit the hero she'd imagined. "Then you buried yourself in your work."

"It's solace." As if that explained everything.

Which, she supposed, it did. "And you swore off relationships."

"Easier that way. Less complicated."

She'd be wise to heed the warning. Somehow he managed to keep his emotions boxed off. Which she didn't.

"Since it's the night for revelations…"

She laughed. "I have nothing to tell. As you overheard, and reacted to, my father says I'm too emotional." She looked away for a moment. "He's not wrong. I think with my heart and that gets me into trouble. Maybe I'm more like my mom than I want to admit. That might be what frustrates my dad."

"Look sweetheart. We both know your dad is seriously fucked up. His reactions have nothing to do with you. Could be that your mother behaves as she does because it's the only means she has of getting a reaction out of him."

Insightful. But she didn't know how accurate his guess was. "As far as I remember, it's always been this way. Now that I think about it, I don't know what motivated them to ever get married. Well, other than I guess my grandfather encouraged her to get married and raise a family." Had she been a good girl, just like Morgan was attempting to be?

He brushed a stray lock of hair from her forehead. "Listen to me, Golden Eyes. You're fine the way you are."

"I made a fool of myself with you that night…at Joe and Noelle's wedding."

"I disagree completely." He shook his head. "You were perfect. But there was hurt in your eyes, and there was nothing more that I wanted than to make you believe in yourself again."

He'd been transparent. How could she be any less so? "My former boyfriend is named Dirk." Even now the memory still hurt. "He came home one night after being at a tradeshow smelling as if he'd bathed in gardenias or something like that."

"Not your scent."

"And lipstick on his collar. He said they'd all partied together to celebrate the show being a success. Nothing happened, except some drinking. I was making too much out of it, being emotional." She sighed as the memory resurfaced. "Maybe I was. But I burst into tears." Just like she had after Kane walked away. "The next day he said he couldn't deal with my histrionics."

"Is that what he called your normal reaction?"

She nodded. "Then he kicked me out."

"Bastard didn't deserve you."

"I stayed a couple of nights with Noelle, but she was getting ready to move in with Joe, so I ended up at a hotel while I searched for a place to live."

"Piece of work."

"And that's when you came on the scene." She'd been at her worst, raw and vulnerable. And maybe he'd been the smarter one. If she'd made love with him, would she have fallen for the unavailable special-forces operator? And what then? Cried when he left and hoped he remembered her?

She was stronger now, more resilient, better able to deal with the fact that he'd soon walk out of her life. And maybe they'd never meet again.

"About ready to go inside?"

"I think I'm getting a little overheated." And maybe a little sad.

She moved to a different section of the tub where she could lift her upper body out of the water, keeping her back to the yard.

Proud and glorious, he climbed out, using his hands to shuck the water from his skin. He didn't bother with a robe and instead picked up hers and held it for her. Moments later, she was wrapped in its plushness.

He held the door while she entered the living room. Then he instructed Polly to begin the nighttime shutdown.

"Good night, Morgan." There was silence for a few moments. *"And Cranky Bastard."*

"That's it. Calling Bonds tomorrow."

"I find her charming."

"Do all females stick together?"

In his suite, still naked, his cock hard, he glanced at her. "I'm going to shower. Feel free to rinse off. I'll meet you back here when you're ready."

She nodded her agreement.

"Have you ever experimented with anal penetration?"

Scandalized, she blinked. How did he always throw her off like this? Did he do it intentionally?

"Hmm?"

"A little, and it was a long time ago." He thrilled her, frightened her. And it gave her comfort to know she had a safe word.

"Be wearing that fancy negligee I selected."

That tone was back in his voice, the one that commanded her instant obedience.

"And I want the vibrator plugged in on your side of the bed."

Heat, that had nothing to do with the water they'd been in, suffused her.

"Any questions?"

"No, Sir."

Ten minutes later, she joined him. He had a small bottle of lubricant next to the bed, and the pillows had been removed.

She exhaled a slow breath to settle herself.

"The nightgown is everything I imagined. And more."

Would she ever get used to his compliments?

"Now take it off."

His voice was gruff with implacable command. Always the Dom. *Her Dom.*

"Please kneel on the mattress near the headboard and hold onto the posts."

Once she was in position, exposed as he demanded, he squirted a jelly-type lube onto his fingers and picked up the vibrator with his other hand.

He slid his slick fingers around her pussy, making her jerk from the sensuality. When she was moving against him, ready for an orgasm, he pressed the vibrator to her pussy on a pulse setting until she began to beg.

"Tell me what you want."

"Sir! I need something constant. You're driving me mad."

"Say no more."

When he changed the setting, he also increased the speed.

She needed all of her self-control to keep her hands where he demanded.

"Come for me, sweetheart."

He gave her an orgasm, and while she was still writhing, he inserted a finger into her rear, plunging it in and out while manipulating the vibe.

Dropping her head forward, she screamed as he brought her wave after wave of ecstasy.

Finally, gasping, drenched with perspiration, unable to hold herself upright any longer, he took mercy on her.

After turning off the toy, he helped her to lie down.

"I'll be right back." He dropped a kiss on her forehead, a self-satisfied smile on his face.

A couple of minutes later, he returned with a warm, damp washcloth for her. No man would ever be able to compare to him.

Then he joined her on the bed, slipped a condom on, and made sweet, sweet love to her.

Afterward, he pulled her against him, snuggling her tight beneath the blankets.

Suddenly her ringing phone shattered the quiet and the peace she'd finally found.

More than tempted to ignore the summons, she sighed. Given the time, it might be her mother complaining about the way the dogs had been taken care of or something.

Before she reached a decision, the device fell silent. *Problem solved.*

Then it trilled again.

She opened her eyes again, frustrated. If her mother was indeed demanding Morgan's attention, this pattern would continue until she answered or set the volume to silent.

Resolved, she reached for the annoying thing to glance at the screen.

Holden Headquarters.

"Who is it?"

"Work. And I have no idea why they'd call me at this hour." She pushed the button to connect the call. "Morgan Holden."

"Ms. Holden, this is Kevin Geery at headquarters. I apologize for the interruption, but we're unable to reach your father."

Which didn't explain why they were calling her. She was so far down the corporate ladder as to not register.

"As per protocol, we tried Harold Loughton, then your brother, Pierce Holden."

Did he even know he was on the list?

"There seems to have been a break-in."

"Break-in?" She frowned.

"Alarm sounded on the seventh floor."

Where her office was housed.

Beside her, Kane snatched up his phone, and she put hers on speaker so he didn't miss any details.

"We responded, and your office door was unlocked. Our rounds indicated it was locked earlier in the evening."

Dread coiled in her stomach.

"Our records don't indicate that you've been here since you left Friday after work."

And at this time of the night, there would have been a security guard on duty that she would have had to pass. "That's correct."

"Then I'm afraid to tell you, Ms. Holden, it appears someone has been in your office."

"Not the housekeeping service?" Frantically she searched for an explanation that made sense.

"They were in the building yesterday."

Kane pointed toward the door, indicating they should head out. Then he walked to her closet.

"My father is flying back from New Orleans this evening. Please keep trying to reach him and Mr. Loughton. In the meantime, I'm on my way."

"Yes, ma'am."

The phone slipped from her nerveless fingers.

CHAPTER SEVEN

HAWKEYE

K ane tossed some of her clothing onto the bed. Then he typed a message before pocketing his phone.

In less than five minutes, they were underway, and when he reached Sixth Avenue, he opened up the throttle, driving about nine miles over the speed limit. Fast, but hopefully within parameters that wouldn't attract the attention of law enforcement.

"Call him back and ask him to prepare a log of everyone who's been in the building since Friday."

Grateful for something to do, she grabbed her phone and made the call.

"Better if he can email it."

"So you can send it to Inamorata. Good thinking."

During the drive, she continued to dial both her mother and her father's numbers to no avail. "I don't suppose you told Inamorata I need to talk to Pierce."

"She's been advised."

Unlike last night, he didn't call back right away.

When they arrived, a security guard walked over to unlock the main door.

"Act confident," Kane whispered in her ear.

That was so much easier with him by her side.

She showed her badge, and he wrote down the number. Ordinarily she'd need it to enter her office.

"And yours, sir?"

With a smile, she glanced at his badge. "Dan... This is my husband, Kane. I'm sure you understand that he has no intention of letting me out at this time of night by myself."

"That's—"

"Do we need to sign something? A log?"

"Uh... Yeah." He walked behind a desk and pulled out a clipboard.

They each scrawled their names.

Then the guard hesitated for a moment. "How about a driver's license, sir?"

"Sure." He pulled out his wallet and read the number to the man.

She knew what Kane was thinking: antiquated. Maybe even adorable. "Please inform Mr. Geery we'll meet him at my office. He's expecting me."

Then, shoulders squared, she led the way to the elevator.

Once inside, she dropped her shoulders against the back wall and sighed. "I can't believe we just waltzed right in."

"Scary. But you did well. Being confident goes a long way."

As the elevator lights illuminated one by one, her anxiety notched up.

The moment the carriage slid to a stop, he looked at her. "If I tell you to do something, please do so without argument."

"You're freaking me out."

"I need you thinking clearly."

She half expected him to take her hand or guide her down

the hallway, but then it occurred to her. Kane had to keep his hand free in case he needed to pull his gun.

How had this dizzying set of events become her life?

Geery was waiting outside her office, along with a female security officer.

Drawing on the fact she was the owner's daughter, telling herself she had every right to be here, Morgan offered her hand. "Thank you for calling us." Then she indicated Kane. "My husband, Kane Patterson."

The two men shook hands.

"I assume you have the log I requested?"

"Sent it to your email about two minutes ago."

"Thank you." What would someone who knew what they were doing say? "My father and I appreciate your efficiency." *Now what?*

Thankfully Kane stepped in, taking away the indecision. "Has anyone touched the doorknob?"

"I did," Geery affirmed. "Cleaning crew yesterday, probably. Not uncommon for our team to do a cursory check on our rounds."

"I assume they badged into work, so their names will be on the list my wife has?"

He nodded. "Yes, sir."

"Mind if we go in?"

How could he be so cool when her heart was racing, at least double the speed it usually did.

Geery used his master pass to unlock the office. Then he stepped aside.

They entered, and she immediately halted, wide-eyed as her nightmare shifted and morphed, getting worse and worse.

"Everything look okay, Ms. Holden?"

"Fine." Her voice cracked on the outright lie.

"Are you sure, darling?"

"Yes. Can't imagine why anyone would want to come in here."

Geery's walkie-talkie squawked, and he keyed the thing, then stepped back into the hallway.

"What the fuck?" Kane whispered, placing a reassuring hand on her shoulder.

"There's a package on the credenza. It wasn't there when I left."

"Quick thinking."

"You two okay here?" Geery asked. "I need to check something out."

She and Kane both turned toward the man.

"Getting notifications on a couple more offices. I'm beginning to think maybe we're having an electrical problem or programming glitch. Gonna go check it out."

Morgan nodded. "You'll keep me informed, Mr. Geery?"

"Yes, ma'am."

When she was alone with Kane, she studied him. "You wouldn't happen to know anything about the sudden glitch, would you?"

He shrugged. "Maybe."

Even though the sound came from a great distance, the man's communication system pinged him again.

"It looks as if our Mr. Geery's going to have a busy night."

"We needed to be alone." His words weren't an apology.

Machiavelli had nothing on him.

"I want you to send the file to Inamorata." He rattled off the email address.

"Of course." While she was occupied with that, he slipped on a pair of gloves, then dusted the doorknob with some sort of powder before pressing clear tape to the surface.

His jacket was obviously as well equipped as Logan's had been. "Lifting fingerprints?"

"More knowledge from your podcasts?"

She watched him use a small brush to wipe away the excess powder.

Then, with his foot, he closed the door, sealing them inside. "You deployed some quick thinking tonight, Ms. Holden."

"It just doesn't seem to be enough."

"We make a good team."

The truth was, without him at her side, she wouldn't have been so competent.

"Let me dust that box to see if we have anything useable." He shrugged. "Not likely."

A few, agonizingly slow minutes later, he offered her a pair of gloves and a pocketknife. "Unless you want me to open it."

She nodded. "Go ahead." Her hands were shaking so hard she doubted it would be possible to slice through the sealing tape.

With a single swipe, using surgical precision, he had the flaps parted.

With a single glance, she looked at the contents. It was a beautiful, glass-beaded clutch, one of her mother's favorites. "My mom's. Or one identical to it." But what were the odds? Laurel had paid a mint for the colorful, jungle-themed purse with a brass clasp.

Something else that had been taken during the break-in?

"Do you want me to take it out?"

"Are you guessing there's something inside?"

That he didn't answer told her all she needed to know.

Carefully he lifted out the bag and placed it upright on her desk. "Your call, sweetheart." This time, his endearment wasn't sensual or teasing; it was soft and protective. "You can step out of the room if you want. Or we can leave it unopened."

Someone had gone to a tremendous amount of effort to get it to her. "I need to know."

With a nod, he parted the clasp.

Instantly she recognized her mom's handwriting on a scrap of paper.

Insurance. Just in case. Your brother will know what to do with this.

But there appeared to be nothing else inside.

Now she was more lost than ever. Then she exhaled. "There's a secret compartment in one side."

With a nod, Kane felt around until he located it, then pulled out a small envelope with her name on the outside, also written in mother's large, sweeping script.

The note inside had obviously come off a printer. The typeface appeared chaotic, and the ink was an unnerving blood red.

A list of names appeared, one beneath the other: Harold Loughton, all the dogs, Pierce, hers, her father, her aunt, then finally her mother.

"Fucking damnation."

"What the hell is this?" Frowning, she shook her head and looked at Kane. "And what does it mean?"

"I don't want to hazard a guess."

She grabbed his wrist. "Knock it off. You damn well know something."

His eyes were narrowed. "We need to move."

"Kane, no. I need to talk to my mom." Once more, she tried and again received voice mail. Same with her father's number.

"Morgan, I mean it." He dropped the notes in the bag and placed it back in the box. After removing his gloves, he spoke again. "Let's go."

"Wait. Give me a minute." She took a cell phone picture of both notes, then sent the images to Pierce.

Drumming his fingers on his thigh, radiating impatience, he looked at her. "Those going to Inamorata?"

"My brother."

"Shoot them to her as well."

She should have thought of that.

His phone pinged, and he pulled it out. Looking at it rather than her, he instructed her to grab the box.

His fingers were inches from the doorknob when he froze, then slowly lowered his hand.

When he looked over his shoulder at her, his jaw was set in a hard line. What had he just read?

Morgan barely recognized the harsh man standing in front of her.

"What floor is Harold Loughton's office on?"

Her heart slamming against her chest, she frowned. "What's going on?"

He hesitated for a moment, and she was afraid he wouldn't answer.

"Listen, Kane. You may be a badass operative who's focused on what he's doing. But I'm right here with you, and I have a right to know." Morgan brought up her chin in determination. She was damn sick and tired of men acting as if they knew best. "I'm not answering any more questions until you talk to me. This is my life we're dealing with."

As if it were against his better judgment, and he needed to act rather than have a conversation, he exhaled a jagged sigh. "He badged in on Friday afternoon. And there's no record of him leaving the premises."

The world swam beneath her.

"I need you to stay calm."

Drawing a breath, she squeezed her eyes shut.

"You can do this." He modulated his tone before continuing, using the one that compelled her to do anything he wished. "Hang with me, Morgan."

Drinking in his reassurance, she looked at him. "The bigwigs are on the tenth floor."

"Would you like to stay here?"

Alone? Wondering what was going on? Jumping at every sound? "No, thank you. Should I notify Geery that we're headed that way?"

With a tight nod, he took her elbow and headed for the door, bypassing the elevator in favor of the stairs.

He took them two at a time, and even though she had to jog to keep up, she didn't ask him to slow down.

They emerged from the stairwell to find Geery and the female security guard already there.

Kane took command. "We need to get in that office."

When Geery looked to her for guidance, Morgan nodded, not having a clue what was going on. "Please do as he asks."

Geery pressed his master key card to a pad and a soft click indicated the lock had opened. The man opened the door. "Shit."

Kane moved in front of her, blocking her view. A terrible stench assailed her, making her reel.

Geery stepped aside.

"Stay here with my wife," he told the female security guard while he donned gloves and strode inside the executive's suite.

Brutal cold chilling her all the way to the bone, Morgan stood there shaking as shock and reality suffocated her.

The security guard next to her was pale, unmoving, staring at the wall.

Moments later, Kane emerged from the room, eyes bleak. "We're out of here." His jaw was set in an uncompromising line.

Everything about him radiated controlled tension. The way he pursed his lips made it clear that she could argue with him at her peril.

But she was equally as determined. "As the only Holden onsite, I have obligations to the company." She gulped. "And to Harold." Dread threatened to drown her again, and she had to struggle to keep it at bay. "There are a million details. And... Hell." She blew out a breath. "I need to call the police."

"Geery has already handled that."

"But—"

"Listen, Morgan. You've got two options." He leaned close to her, a breath away so that no one else could overhear what he had to say. "You can walk. Or I'm throwing you over my shoulder. We're getting the fuck out of here. And we're leaving in the next five seconds."

The box clutched tight, she looked into his obsidian eyes. So much was there—resolve, understanding. Something was happening that she didn't understand.

"That's it." Giving her no more time to react, he rushed her toward the elevator. "Faster than the stairs."

"Ms. Holden!" Geery called.

"My wife is understandably distressed."

That was a ridiculous understatement.

"The police can call her if they need to. She's done all she's doing for tonight."

Once they were inside the compartment with the doors closed, she looked at him. "Kane..." Where to begin? Not that she could have done much good, but she should have stayed. Wasn't that the right thing to do? "What the hell is happening here?"

"I'll explain as soon as I can."

"Harold's dead." There could be no other explanation for everything that had just happened and the putrid stench stinging her nose. "Isn't he?" She'd had no doubt, but Kane's pursed lips provided the confirmation she really hadn't wanted. It made it so much more real. "How...? What happened? A heart attack or something?" It had to be, or at least that's what she hoped.

"No."

"It wasn't..." She gulped. "Natural causes?"

"I wish it were."

"Suicide?"

When he didn't answer, she squeezed her eyes shut.

Her mind raced, going back over every event that had happened since Saturday: the break-ins, her missing computer, her mother's purse. Kane's unrelenting sense of urgency.

Suddenly her brain froze, grinding to a halt on an awful, horrific realization.

Harold's name was on the list her mother had sent her. Along with hers, and Pierce's.

Her entire world splintered, and she grabbed for the brass railing so she didn't collapse. "Kane?" The word barely emerged.

Instantly he slid a supporting arm around her waist. "I know what you're thinking. And you can't let it consume you. Right now we have to keep moving. Be strategic."

How was that possible when her world lay around her like shattered glass?

Nausea roiled through her.

"More than ever, Morgan, you need to compartmentalize. You've earned the right to fall apart, and I'll be there for you when you do. But hold it at bay. Think about getting to the vehicle. Geery won't be able to catch up to us, but nothing is faster than a walkie-talkie. So the security guard in the lobby may attempt to stop us. Keep walking. Don't respond to anything he says, unless it's in vague terms."

She nodded.

"If he attempts to get physical, I'll handle it."

No doubt he would.

The button for the bottom floor lit, signaling they would be on ground level in mere seconds.

Drawing her a little closer, he dropped a kiss on the top of her head, and she'd had no idea how much she'd needed the silent—if unrealistic—promise that everything would be okay.

Before the doors were fully opened, he kept his arm in place and guided her across the lobby.

As expected, Dan, the guard from earlier, stood there, a hand on his baton. "Mr. Geery would like to talk to you."

Kane kept her moving, navigating around the man, and she was grateful for Kane's coaching. The good manners she'd been raised with would have required her to stop and maybe try to explain herself.

"Ms. Holden. I must insist—"

The heavy glass door they'd entered on the way in was now locked.

Instantly Kane pivoted, hustling her through the space toward the area of the stairs and the emergency exit.

Was that part of his strategic thinking? Always having a backup plan?

The man started to chase them.

"Go!" Kane insisted. "Straight to the car."

"I can't." She shook her head. "Not without you."

"I'll be three seconds behind you. If you're able to run, do so." He shoved on the metal bar to open the exit. The alarm blared, and he pushed her from the building.

The thick door slammed behind her, leaving her with no way to get back in the building.

Disoriented as to which direction to take, she forced in a breath. Think. *Think.* She would never again criticize people who did seemingly ridiculous things while under stress.

Knowing that Kane was counting on her and not wanting to slow him down, she glanced around for a street sign. Once she figured out where she'd emerged, she dashed toward the front of the building.

A handful of seconds later, he caught up with her and fell in step next to her.

She was breathing fast, slowing him down, and she hated that. But he made no attempt to rush her any faster.

"Geery may get outside before we do."

Kane hadn't mentioned Dan. Did that mean the man was incapacitated?

"If any attempt is made to delay us, I want you in the vehicle with the doors locked. Understand?"

Even if that meant he wasn't inside with her. Reluctantly she nodded. Then realizing he might not be able to see her in the dark, she spoke. "Yes."

From half a block away, he unlocked the vehicle and started the engine.

As they neared, the female security guard was attempting to turn the key in the lock.

The woman didn't appear to want to accost them, and Morgan didn't blame her, especially if she'd been witness to the way Kane had dealt with Dan.

Still, she valiantly exited the building.

With a clipped voice, Kane spoke to Morgan. "You know what to do." Then he approached the guard to stand directly in front of her, giving Morgan the time and space to scramble into the vehicle.

When he spoke, his voice was more threatening than anything Morgan had ever heard. "Ma'am, I'm guaranteeing you, you don't want to do this."

Morgan dropped the box onto the floor as she pulled the door closed and hit the switch for the locks.

Kane took a step closer to the female security guard, then

placed his hands on her shoulders and turned her back toward the building.

She stopped.

Even through the sealed vehicle, she heard Kane speak. "Last chance to go home with all your limbs intact."

As she stood there frozen, he hurried toward the SUV.

Relieved, Morgan hit the switch to let him inside.

This time he paid little attention to traffic laws as he burned rubber toward his home.

She recalled the way the guard had stared, unable to act, as they'd stood outside Harold's office in the eerie silence, the lack of sound so overwhelming it seemed to echo.

"Would you have really hurt that woman?"

"I gave her a chance to make the right decision." He looked at her pointedly. "You're my obligation, sweetheart. Nothing—and no one—will stand in my way."

Once he was on Sixth Avenue, he pressed a button on the dash to call Inamorata. "You're on speaker."

"Acknowledged."

"Loughton is dead."

She didn't answer.

"Double-tap."

Her entire body now numb, Morgan collapsed against the seatback.

She knew what that meant. Two shots from a gun. Because he was in his office, it was likely at close range and to his head. The first bullet would be to incapacitate, the second to ensure he was dead.

A double-tap was no accident. He was the victim of a targeted assassination.

"Need someone to meet me at my place. Got prints that need to be processed."

"Enroute."

Then she was consumed by an awful, empty silence that

allowed her too much time to think. "My life is in danger." Along with every member of her family, and even the pets. God. Who could be such a damn animal?

And more, why?

"It seems to be."

"You haven't sugar-coated anything so far." Oh God, her voice held a frantic, fragile edge. "Why start now?"

He reached across the compartment to take her hand. "Evidence suggests that. But your guess is far from a foregone conclusion."

She wished she could believe that. What other option was there?

"And even if we were positive—which we're not—it doesn't mean anything. Hawkeye is working on it—"

As if that's enough. "What about law enforcement?"

"Part of Inamorata's job is to interface with the various agencies."

Did he always use such vague language? Or was she just on the verge of hysteria? "Like the local police department?"

"Yes. And the FBI."

"FBI?"

"Look, sweetheart…"

"I'm not falling apart." She still had a hold of her sanity, even if the threads were unraveling fast.

"Anything I say is conjecture."

"My mind is filling in the blanks. Whatever you have to say can't be as bad."

He gripped the steering wheel tighter. Was that his way of disagreeing with her?

Finally he spoke. "Plenty of criminals use a double-tap." He glanced in the rearview mirror. "Along with organized crime groups."

Holy shit. "The…*mob?*" She turned, trying to search his features. "You think Harold was taken out by a mob hit?"

"I didn't say that."

Maybe not in so many words, but that was the implication.

Around and around, like a dizzying carousel, her thoughts spun. Why...? And how was her family connected?

They reached his home in record time, and even when they were sealed inside along with a team from Hawkeye, she couldn't relax.

At some point, Kane pressed a glass of wine into her hand. Inamorata took custody of Laurel Holden's five-thousand-dollar purse with the note inside. And her parents were still unreachable. And even Hawkeye had no information on their whereabouts.

Time blurred among the dizzying number of questions, of Kane recounting events and turning over the prints he'd lifted.

All that meant that no one was in charge of the corporate offices.

Doubting Kane would approve of what she was going to do, she walked down the hall into his workout room and placed a call to Geery.

"The police are looking for you. You need to give them a statement."

"I'm fully prepared to do so." Still, she was the boss—at least for now. "Is there a procedure for shutting down the business for a day or two? Allowing employees to work from home?"

"We have emergency protocols, yes." His voice was tight. Polite but obviously pissed off at the way she and Kane had handled things. "They're often used for inclement weather."

"Activate them until further notice. No one is allowed on campus without an escort and permission from a Holden."

"Yes, ma'am."

She had no idea what she was doing or if she was making

the right choices. But who knew how long the crime scene unit would be onsite?

Gossip spread fast, and employees were sure to have millions of questions that she couldn't answer. Under the circumstances, would anyone get any work done? "It's been a rough night, Mr. Geery. Thank you." Morgan stopped herself from going on; otherwise she'd end up apologizing for the way she and Kane behaved.

He'd taken steps to protect her, and she appreciated that.

When she returned to the kitchen, Inamorata and Kane were both seated at the table and indicated she was welcome to join them.

Not that she'd be able to stay still.

As she slid into a chair, he reached a hand across to her. "The police will want to speak with both of us."

"I expected that." *Will the day ever end?*

Inamorata leaned forward. "I recommend you have a lawyer with you."

"A..." *What?* "Why?"

"It's always advisable."

"Are you serious? No one can actually think that I had anything to do with this."

"They'll ask dozens of questions and try to trip you up. Circle back around. Repeat what they said in a slightly different way until you begin to doubt yourself."

As exhausted as she was, maybe it was a good idea to have someone with her.

"Do you have an attorney?"

"As if." Morgan gave a slight laugh. "As I keep saying, I'm boring. Nothing ever happens to me. I go to work; I come home. There's not even a speeding ticket on my record. So no, I don't have anyone on speed dial."

"Would you like a recommendation?"

Since she had no clue where to begin, she agreed. "Thank you."

"I'll make a call. Excuse me."

When she was momentarily alone with Kane, she pressed her fingers against her tired eyes. "What about you?"

"Mine's on the way."

"You're old hat at this."

"Comes with the job."

The small glimpse she'd had of his life was enough to tell her it wasn't for her. They lived in separate worlds, and she liked her insulated existence. "Do we need to go to the police station?"

"They'll come to us."

"Okay."

Pierce finally called, and the relief that rushed through her was palpable. As if he were a lifeline, she answered.

"You okay, little sis?"

There was tension in his vocal cords that she'd never heard before. "The last couple of days have been awful."

"It has to have been hell for you." He blew out a breath. "I've been in contact with Inamorata, and I'm heading back from Nevada. You're doing great. No one could do it better."

Aware of Kane's gaze on her, she stood and paced as she spoke, wanting some semblance of privacy.

Hardly slowing down, Pierce went on. "I'm sure you're aware that what you found is probably a hit list. Potentially organized crime. No idea why we're on it. Yet."

A part of her appreciated his bluntness; another part recoiled from the harsh reality.

"Stay where you are, okay?"

As if she had any idea what to do otherwise.

"I'm going to move Ella to a safe house."

Her knees wobbled.

"I don't want anyone looking for me and finding her."

Dear God. "I'm so sorry." How was it possible for this nightmare to become worse by the minute? "You should go with her, Pierce."

"Forget it." As she expected, he scoffed. "No matter what either of you say. My family's at risk, and I'm not going to sit back and do nothing."

Always the protector.

"You're safe with Patterson, but if you want to go to the safe house, I'll make it happen."

Maybe she was more like her brother than she realized. She wanted to stay where she was. "Not right now."

"Consider it."

"I will. Have you been able to get hold of Mom or Dad? I haven't."

"No."

She gave him a rundown of what actions she'd taken at headquarters. "You can take over anytime. Your name is higher on the list."

"No fucking chance. You're doing fine."

All she wanted to do was shut it down and let her dad deal with it when he returned. *If* he returned.

In less than half an hour, her lawyer arrived—Billy Dawson, a retired judge, well-regarded in the community, in the District Attorney's office, and among police officers. Even if she'd had all the time in the world, she couldn't have made a better choice.

The next hour with the police passed in a blur of confusion and an unwelcome reliving of the gruesome events that had happened at work.

When they finally left, she thanked Billy. Inamorata was right about their questioning that felt more like an interrogation. She was so exhausted, overwrought from everything she'd been through, that she was no longer able to keep her thoughts straight. Her attorney had stepped in on numerous occasions to redirect them or tell her not to answer. "Having you here helped."

He offered his card. "Call anytime. And don't talk to anyone with a badge without me there."

After he shook hands with Inamorata, he left.

Since Kane was still being questioned in his office, she walked into the kitchen to pour a fresh glass of wine. Then it occurred to her to offer Ms. Inamorata one

"Thank you, no."

How did she still look perfect at this time of the night? Or morning was more like it.

"May I give you a piece of advice?"

"Please."

"Get some rest. Take a bath. Try to unwind."

"Because the shitshow isn't over?"

"That's one way to put it." Inamorata stood and grabbed her bag. "I'll be in touch tomorrow. Don't hesitate to call."

She took a drink of the wine. "Nothing personal, but I hope I have no reason to contact you ever again."

"You're not the only one." She gave a tight nod. In the foyer, she hesitated. "Hello, Polly. Open the door."

Computer—Chief of Staff—was too smart to argue back.

Then, deciding to be equally as intelligent, Morgan took Inamorata's advice and headed upstairs to soak in the bathtub. Polly must have turned the heat up, because the water was already warm when Morgan turned the knob.

Once it was full, she tipped her head back and closed her eyes. Sleep would be a long time coming tonight, if it ever arrived.

But at some point, the mental and physical cost must have been too high for her body to deal with.

The next thing she knew, Kane was helping her from the tub, wrapping her in a towel, and carrying her while she pressed her cheek to his chest.

After placing her in bed, he tucked her beneath the blankets.

The last thing she remembered was being pulled against his hard, nurturing body.

Until reality destroyed the peace.

CHAPTER EIGHT

HAWKEYE

"Hey, Golden Eyes."

Morgan gathered the blankets and yanked them over her head. "Go away." She meant it. On one hand, she could count the number of hours of sleep she'd had since Friday night.

Despite her grip on the coverings, light seeped in. Then the scent of sugar and fresh-brewed coffee filled the air.

Kane?

What day was it?

Suddenly dreadful memories swamped her, chasing away the sleep she'd been getting.

Next to her, the mattress dipped down.

Surrendering to the inevitable, she sat up, blinking the world into focus.

He was holding a cup bearing the logo of her favorite coffee shop. "For me?"

"I don't know who else would drink it."

For a moment, the world seemed normal, though it was anything but. She appreciated his gesture.

With a grateful smile, she accepted the offering.

After her first sip, happiness and deliciousness rolled into one, she was awake enough to ask a logical question. "How did it get here?"

"I asked Inamorata to pick it up."

"That was thoughtful." Then she frowned. "Wait. She's back?" Morgan looked around, searching for a clock "What time is it?"

"A little before seven."

No wonder she was groggy. "So the obvious question is why."

"Two reasons. Your parents are back in town."

She snatched up her phone, but there were no messages and no missed calls.

"They arrived around three a.m."

Neither of them returned a single call or text, and that didn't make any sense. Her dad had to know about the decisions she'd made at Holden, and he hadn't questioned them?

"And the FBI wants to talk to you."

Her stomach plunged. "About what?"

Before answering, he tucked wayward strands of her hair behind her ear. A moment of tenderness in a world gone mad. "The list of names your mom sent you."

"The hit list, you mean?"

This time he didn't caution that she was jumping to conclusions. And she wasn't sure which was worse—the truth or planting enough doubt that she believed she could be wrong.

"Thought you might want some time to dress or shower before they arrive."

She shrieked. "You mean the feds are on their way *now?*"

"Inamorata took the liberty of calling Billy."

"But…I'm not ready."

"Be grateful you got any heads-up. This morning, a lot of

people aren't that lucky. Warrants are being executed in several states right now."

"Warrants?" Morgan shivered.

"At multiple businesses."

She had to know—*had to...* "Including ones owned by Holden?"

"I'm not privy to the details."

"You have a guess."

Though he hesitated, he finally answered. "I wouldn't rule it out."

At least he got points for honesty.

In a zombielike state, she showered, dressed, put on some mascara, and tucked her hair into a bun…the best she could do with the time she had.

She checked her phone. Pierce had messaged that he arrived at headquarters a few hours ago and was catching some sleep and would be in touch soon. Having him nearby was reassuring.

When she came down the stairs, cup in hand, she hesitated.

Two people, a man and woman, both in suits, stood next to each other.

The woman, she recognized from the evening at the Reserve. As she'd sat at the far end of the bar, Kane had identified her as a cop.

"I'm Special Agent Harwood"—she indicated the man—"and this Special Agent Simms, Federal Bureau of Investigations."

Both showed their identification, and Harwood offered a business card. Another for her collection.

"We have a few questions, if you don't mind."

"As long as you answer a few for me, beginning with what the hell is going on?"

"We're hoping you can help us with that."

In the kitchen—Inamorata and Kane nearby and Billy seated at Morgan's side, the agents across from them—a long, complex interview began. The questions centered mostly on her father's business, the galleries and auction house in particular.

"I wish I could help you. Dad has no interest in a woman serving at the highest levels of his corporation, even his daughter. I'm in marketing for the clothing boutiques, and I've never done anything for those divisions."

The questioning went on and on, around and around, until Billy rapped his knuckles on the table. "That's it for today."

Harwood leveled him with a hard stare. "Just a couple more questions."

"Is my client under arrest?"

Arrest? Her entire body stiffened. His question couldn't be serious. Frantically she looked at him, then at Kane who held her gaze, letting her know he was going nowhere.

"Agents?" Billy looked from one to the other.

"Of course not." Harwood spoke for both of them.

"In that case, I'm sure you agents have something useful to do with your time." Then he stood, indicating in no uncertain terms that the meeting was over.

With a tight acknowledgment, Harwood followed suit.

Like Inamorata before her, Harwood told Morgan to give them a call if she thought of anything else. "I will. But before you go…are you doing anything about the hit list?"

Harwood and Simms exchanged glances, and neither replied.

"I assume you're aware of it?"

Harwood nodded. "At the moment, we're investigating it, ma'am."

"That's a better use of your time than harassing my

client." Billy smiled in a way that didn't take the heat out of his statement.

Once the lawyer and the federal agents had gone, Morgan stood and faced Inamorata and Kane. "Seems you need to catch me up on a few things. You can start talking anytime."

Inamorata gave a curt nod. "Patterson?"

Kane shifted. "Shall we have a seat?"

Would she be glad for that?

As if he were giving a military briefing, he provided facts and didn't elaborate on details.

"Last night, Hawkeye turned over your note to the FBI. Harwood works in the OCS—Organized Crime Section."

"Because…?" That they'd give the information to the police made sense to her. But why the feds?

A piece of the puzzle clicked into place. The assassination of Harold Loughton. Was it a Mafia hit?

From a great distance, Kane's voice cut through her haze, and she realized he was still speaking.

"Morgan?"

Her heart raced, making it impossible to concentrate. "Sorry."

The photograph of the dogs? We got a hit off a fingerprint on the back. And we sent it over to Harwood. Though she was reluctant to part with the information, she informed us it belonged to a suspected Mafia soldier."

As if she could stave off the doom closing around her, she hugged herself.

Inamorata picked up the story. "We believe it was intentional."

Though Morgan knew nothing about these kinds of things, it was hard to disagree. The frame had been facedown as if someone wanted to send a message. "Why the hell would the mob be threatening my family?"

"We'd all like to know."

Her phone chimed. Glad for the distraction, but wishing her hand wasn't shaking, she picked it up.

The name on the screen made her blink. "It's my mom."

When she tapped on the message icon and saw it had been sent to both her and Pierce.

She read it aloud. *You're needed at the house urgently.*

Inamorata and Kane exchanged glances, and Kane reached his hand toward Morgan. "It's your call. If you want to go, we will. The house is still under surveillance."

"I want answers." As she was standing, her brother responded to their mother's text. *Rolling.*

Then he sent her a personal one. *See you there.*

After telling Kane to keep her advised, Inamorata left.

Then they were alone once more. "Are you ready?" he asked.

For what? Wishing she had any idea what was going on, she grabbed her purse. "Let's go."

The drive took forever, and Pierce pulled in right before they did.

All three of them met in front of the door, and Pierce wrapped her in a massive hug. "I had no idea what they were into."

Even she still couldn't believe it.

After releasing her, Pierce acknowledged his coworker. "Patterson."

"Want me to wait out here?" he asked both of them.

Because so many bizarre events had happened, she wanted the comfort of having him next to her like he had been for every step of the journey so far. "I'd like you to come with me." As she had so many times in the past, she looked to her big brother.

"No objection."

Pierce tried the knob, and it turned, meaning it wasn't locked. The alarm system wasn't blinking.

The men exchanged glances. If the way they both nodded indicated something, they'd reached an unspoken agreement that she had no hope of understanding.

His right hand inside his Hawkeye jacket, Pierce nudged the door open with his foot. After a glance inside, he gave Kane a thumbs-up.

With her sandwiched between the men, they entered.

In a glance, Morgan took in the scene.

Her mother, dressed in black, hair perfectly in place, her makeup done as if she were going to one of her charity meetings, stood with her back to the fireplace, a mimosa in hand. Walter, probably her favorite poodle, was next to her, and Bella snoozed next to him.

The other dogs lay perfectly still near one another, heads on outstretched legs, appearing pensive.

From down the hall, Soren strolled into the room in a crisp, designer suit.

Beyond confused, she looked to Kane. He trailed his fingers down her back as he spoke to the Reserve's owner. "Maybe I shouldn't be surprised to see you here, Soren."

On the other hand, Morgan couldn't be more mystified. Not knowing what to do, how to act, she clutched her purse close to her.

"We haven't met," Pierce said to Soren.

"Soren Addison. Your parents' attorney." The two shook hands.

Attorney? Suddenly Kane's words from that night at the club returned to her.

"The club operates within the confines of the law."

Her immediate thought had been, *Did that mean certain other things did not?*

"Anyone want to tell us why we've been summoned here at this time of the morning?" Pierce asked.

Before anyone could answer, Gerard descended the staircase, also in a suit and his customary Rolex Yacht-Master, looking as if he'd been home for hours rather than recently arriving from outside the country.

"Who the hell are you?" he demanded of Kane.

Pierce responded smoothly. "An associate of mine."

"Jesus." Then he narrowed his eyes as he stared at Morgan. "Let me guess… Your husband?"

"Mr. —"

Refusing to be intimidated any longer, she brought up her hand sharply to interrupt both of them. "He's with me, and he's staying. I don't really give a fuck whether you like it or not." Even though heat rushed through her, so did pride that she'd shattered old patterns by standing up for herself.

"Gerry, *please*. We need to stay focused."

He took a seat and pressed his hands together.

Laurel addressed everyone. "Once this meeting is done, I'm turning myself in to the FBI."

Pierce was silent, assessing.

Morgan rocked back and forth while Kane kept his fingers against the small of her back in silent support.

Searching for understanding, she studied her mom. "But…why?"

"I've been involved in some…unsavory things."

Morgan knitted her eyebrows together in confusion. That her dad would have skirted the law, she believed. But her mother?

"I'm afraid things have gotten out of hand. Tell them, Gerry."

"We had financial difficulties at Holden."

Pierce cursed. "Which Loughton tried to tell me about at the anniversary party."

"You've never had any interest in anything but playing war games, though, have you, son?" Gerard's voice dripped with disdain.

The situation was dire, and their father was still slinging barbs? Through the new lens she'd recently acquired, Morgan saw how messed up her family was.

"And, well…I arranged for some insurance claims. I mean they charge exorbitant premium prices to cover that kind of thing. It's a crime without real harm. Sell the items at the stores and the auction business."

Soren added a few details. "The FBI raided a few businesses this morning, and your mother thought it best to turn herself in. Avoid the press."

She shook her head. "You sent me a package."

"Sorry, darling, if I alarmed you." Laurel waved a hand. "It's the people who would benefit from my scheme."

But the word *insurance* had been on the note.

"I'll be back at the office by noon today," Gerard told Morgan.

He was heartless. And maybe soulless, having no regard for what his wife was facing today.

"Take as much time off as you'd like to, Morgan."

Laurel looked at her kids. "Take care of my babies."

"I'll have her out as soon as possible," Soren promised.

As he reached the door, he turned back. "As soon as the news breaks, your lives will become a paparazzi nightmare."

She, Pierce, and Kane watched them go.

Walter ran to the back door, whimpering.

"She's lying," Morgan said. Every part of her knew it. "Protecting someone."

"Yeah." Pierce plowed a hand into his hair. "She fell on her fucking sword, for the goddamn Mafia. She made herself into a sacrificial lamb."

"What do you mean?"

"Yeah, she was involved. That hit list she sent you… It was supposed to be her way of protecting us. My guess, not that we'll ever be able to prove it, is she got cold feet and told them she wanted out, maybe going as far as to threaten them."

A multitude of emotions pummeling her, she paced. "Makes sense why they didn't want the police involved."

"This is a fucked-up situation. But if she doesn't confess, the mob will stop at nothing to silence everyone connected." Pierce cussed again. "I get why she spent most of her life drinking."

She glanced at the kitchen counter and the million-dollar renovation blueprints sitting there. "Money laundering?"

"Wouldn't be surprised." Pierce turned to Kane. "What do you know about the lawyer?"

"He's been known to represent mob interests."

Pierce nodded. "So he's looking out for them, not my mother."

"Maybe he's doing both."

"You're not defending that piece of shit Soren, are you, Patterson?"

"Hell no. But he's the lawyer on record, and your mother chose him. Either she knew him previously, or he was provided for her."

Reeling from everything going on around her, Morgan exhaled. "Does this mean the threat is over? We don't have to worry about the hit list?"

"It's too soon to say." As always, Kane seemed to hedge his bets. Pragmatic, rather than optimistic.

He was probably right. Now that her family was associated with the mob, would there ever be a way to break free?

"Soren was right about the media circus you're about to enter. Photographers, reporters will be crawling everywhere."

It had to be better than this.

"What are we doing with the babies?" Walter was still near the back door, head tilted, waiting for Laurel's return.

"Hopefully Soren's right, and he'll have her out soon."

"And in the meantime?"

Pierce folded his arms. "I'll take them."

In disbelief, she turned to him. "What? You?"

"I kind of liked Fifi. Or was it Bon Bon?"

"It was Fifi." For the dog it had been love at first sight when she'd met Pierce. "Ella loves them."

"You going to stick around the case now that you don't have to?" Pierce asked Kane. "Powell can wrap it up from here."

Morgan went still, very, very still. "What do you mean?" she asked her brother.

"He got assigned to you Friday night, right? While you and I were both suspects."

"Suspects?" She was repeating what he said, but even after everything life had thrown at her, she couldn't believe what she was hearing.

"Holden?" Kane's voice held a dangerous warning note. "Shut the fuck up."

Pierce scowled. "What's going on?"

Brutal tears stung her eyes. Ignoring her brother, she turned to the man she'd given herself to, body and soul. "That's what I am to you?" She shouldn't be surprised. "So that night, you'd been told to get close to me? Watch me? See if I did anything bad?" Her voice broke. "It was never personal for you." It wasn't a question but a statement of raw, painful truth.

Ever so gently, he placed his hands on her shoulders. "It wasn't like that."

"Did you know I would be at the club?"

He was damningly quiet.

Consumed with hurt that blazed into anger, she lifted her arms to break free from his grip. "When were you going to tell me? Ever? Details are on a need-to-know basis, right? Duty and country."

He exhaled a ragged sigh.

"You two…?"

"Leave us alone," she demanded of her brother. "Go load up the dogs and their kennels."

"Oh fuck. You and Patterson…?"

"Do as the lady says before I lay you out."

"Morgan…"

"Go away, Pierce."

Finally he did, leaving her with Kane and her broken heart. "Tell me where I'm wrong." Then she gave a fractured laugh. "You can't."

She remembered him stepping away to make a call on Friday night before he insisted he wouldn't leave her alone, behaving like a true gentleman and protector.

The truth was, one of her earlier guesses was more accurate. Machiavelli. Didn't matter if she got hurt—again—as long as he did his job. "You know, about one thing, you were totally honest. You told me you were shit at relationships." She gave a brittle laugh. "I should have believed you. That's on me."

Her anguish bubbled out, emotions spilling over despite her frantic attempt to keep them at bay. "How deep does your lack of emotion, your lack of compassion, your lack of trust go? And…when did you know my name was on the hit list?"

"That's irrelevant now."

She balled her hands into fists. *"When did you know?"*

"Golden Eyes—"

"Don't! Don't fucking insult me with your pet names. You knew. And you said nothing. More need to know? Well, here's something you need to know. You hardened me once before, but this time I've learned my lesson. Now get out."

"I'm your ride, Morgan. I'll make sure you get safely wherever you want to go."

"You're off the job, Agent Patterson. From this moment, we're done." Carefully she articulated her next words. "I said get *out.*"

His face ashen, eyes sunken, he nodded. "If you need anything, anything…"

She turned her back.

And the tears fell.

In the end, she caught a ride home from Pierce, ignoring his attempts to make conversation and apologize.

Fortunately Fifi kept insinuating herself between them. Between the road, the traffic, and five dogs, it was easy to keep to herself.

At home, numb, shattered, she packed a bag and pulled on a wig that she'd bought for a Halloween party. Dressed in an oversize puffy jacket, and pulling on a baseball cap, she rode the elevator to the parking garage.

Now that she'd had her name on a mob hit list and someone had burglarized her home, not to mention her mother being in custody, she was now paranoid in ways she couldn't have ever imagined.

While constantly gazing around for threats, she climbed behind the driver's wheel of her SUV, then locked the doors.

With no regrets, she headed for the open highway, and once she was certain she wasn't being followed, she didn't look back.

CHAPTER NINE

HAWKEYE

A month later, bundled in a thick coat against the chilly, ocean wind, Morgan wandered on a secluded, craggy part of the Oregon coast, about as far away from her former life as she could imagine.

After leaving Denver, she'd driven aimlessly for days, ending up at a resort in the mountain town of Park City, Utah, where she'd cut her hair, packed away the wig, bought baseball cap, and ditched her phone for a new one with a different number that she only gave to Pierce and the Carpe Diem Divas.

Next was Las Vegas, where she'd wandered the Strip, eaten a great meal at the Bella Rosa casino, and enjoyed lazing by a magnificent pool before heading into the Southern California desert, ending up in San Diego, then Los Angeles.

Still restless, not wanting to return to the condo that had been broken into, the drama with her mother's arrest and upcoming trial, or haunting memories of Kane, she continued north, heading up the Pacific Coast. For the most part, she enjoyed the drive, stopping whenever she was moved to take pictures of the spectacular shoreline.

It wasn't until she ended up in Brook's Bend, Oregon—a small, vibrant, artistic town that attracted tourists and creatives alike—that she felt compelled to stop.

The town didn't have any brand-name hotels, which suited her. Not that anyone was trying to find her, but she didn't want to take any chances.

At a diner somewhere on the road—Arizona, maybe—an investigative news report on television flashed a picture of Morgan, her parents, and the dogs. Probably taken by a guest at the wedding anniversary celebration.

Uncomfortable, she'd paid her bill and headed out once more, leaving her meal mostly untouched.

For a few nights, she stayed at a Brook's Bend bed-and-breakfast and spent time on the beach—which was definitely unlike the ones she'd traveled to in the Caribbean.

As she wandered through the quaint stores and galleries, she met artists and people like her, who'd been attracted to a place where the continent ended and new dreams began.

Since it was after tourist season, she found a great deal on a long-term vacation rental.

Now, even though the seemingly ever-present cold wind gnawed on her ears, she continued to walk.

The habit—which was now closer to a ritual—brought her a sense of normalcy.

At daybreak, she walked for miles, promising herself she'd forget Kane and move on with her life. Then each morning she woke up realizing she was still lying to herself.

She wasn't sure what healing would even look like. Maybe forgetting she'd seen her name on a hit list? No longer worrying about her mom or what was happening to her? Or maybe no longer being tormented by dreams and relentless images of the unbelievably sexy bodyguard she'd given her heart to?

Maybe that was the crux of her problem.

She'd fallen in love with Kane even though he'd warned her not to.

When he approached her at the club, interrupting her potential scene with Lars, she'd honestly believed he was looking out for her and wanted to connect with her specifically. The spanking had been so real to her, as if they had a connection rather than just being something random between a Top and bottom.

The sense of things being so right, so perfect, had intensified at her parents' home, and then again at his place where he brought her fantasies to life with the vibrator.

But the attraction had been one-sided, and he'd managed to fool her.

Maybe the worst part of the whole thing hadn't been his lies and deceptions, but the fact their BDSM and the sex they'd shared had meant nothing to him.

How mortifying that she gave so freely, and she'd been nothing more than a job to him, someone his boss told him to surveil, even if it meant fucking her.

With his glances and husky, implacable Dominant commands, he hadn't just removed her clothes; he'd stripped off her emotional armor.

The weather turned nastier, and she shoved her hands into her pockets. Wishing she had a pair of gloves, she walked back toward her car.

Once there, she turned on the engine and set the heat to high, willing it to warm up. Since she was from Colorado, she should be accustomed to the cold, but when the wind whipped off the ocean, it seemed to chill her from the inside out.

Which gave her a good reason to seek out Seaside Sips, her new favorite coffee shop.

Since the weather was behaving less than hospitably, keeping people indoors, she found a parking spot directly in front of the store.

After grabbing the backpack that contained her new laptop, she dashed toward the building.

As she did, droplets of rain began to fall, no doubt signaling the arrival of the predicted downpour.

A bell over the entrance jingled when she walked in.

"Hey, MJ!" Rachel, the owner, called out as Morgan struggled to shut the door that the wind attempted to grab out of her hand.

When Rachel had asked for Morgan's name to write on the cup, she automatically decided to use the name she'd selected for the Reserve. While it might not prevent her from eventually getting recognized, the slight change gave her a small measure of much-needed privacy.

Morgan wiped her feet on the mat. "Looks as if it's going to be a rough ride for a few."

"We've got coffee and pastries, though."

"Which is all we need!" Rachel reached for the largest cup. "The usual?"

"Extra shot of espresso, please."

She wrinkled her nose. "You didn't sleep again?"

"Insomnia stinks." But at least she was catching up on some of her reading, books she'd missed over the last few years while trying to impress her boss, and maybe her dad. For all the good that had done her.

As Rachel pulled the shots and steamed the milk, Morgan set up her computer on a small table near the window.

"Extra whipping cream?"

She looked over her shoulder and grinned. Then together they both said, "And double drizzle."

Rachel walked the drink over to her.

"There was no need to do that. I was headed to the counter to pay."

She waved a hand. "This one's on me. Glad for the company."

Across the room, a printer spit out a long piece of paper. "To-go or pick-up order. Maybe delivery," she explained. "Maybe it won't be as quiet as I expected."

"Delivery's an option?" Which meant she didn't have to don a cap or beanie before leaving her cozy cottage.

"Better when it's hot, in my opinion."

"And the whipping cream hasn't all melted." She lifted the lid to lick the frothy confection, just like she had that day with Kane.

God.

What was it going to take to never again have stray thoughts of him wander through her mind, reminding her what she'd lost.

"You okay?"

When she looked up, Rachel was frowning. "You seem to be somewhere else."

"Sorry." With a smile, she attempted to cover the fact she'd meandered back to the past. "I was thinking that going for my walks gets me out of the house." Which she might not do otherwise. "And coming here is my reward."

"And since you've burned off all the calories in advance, it's a win-win situation."

"Exactly." She toasted her acquaintance—*friend?*—with the drink. "It's wonderful, as usual."

Tucked away by herself, she spent the next hour watching travel videos, trying to decide on her next destination.

When she'd left Denver, she'd started taking cash out of ATMs along the way. She had no idea whether the feds would freeze her assets. She'd never done anything wrong, but was guilt by association a thing? The nagging anxiety had her moving on every time she withdrew money or used a credit card.

Her new existence.

How Pierce coped with constant threat and uncertainty, she had no idea.

All the clips she watched were beautiful, designed to entice visitors. But she was comfortable here, which made her wonder if she should search for an apartment or a place with a year-long lease.

But what then?

At some point, she'd need a job. Brook's Bend was nowhere close to a big city where her skills might be in demand. Maybe she could work in one of the quaint shops? Or wait tables? Depending on the cost of her rent, making ends meet might be difficult.

It was smarter to go to a bigger city.

But that's not what she wanted.

Now that her beverage was gone, her tummy grumbled, reminding her it was way past breakfast.

The orders seemed to have slowed down, and Rachel was perched on a stool, bent over a sketchpad.

Grabbing her purse, Morgan went to the counter.

The special was breakfast burritos made by the family that owned El Rancho, the local Mexican-food restaurant that she'd heard good things about. "I need one of those. Well, you know what I mean. Not need. But they look fabulous."

"Which one? The chorizo is amazing."

Anything with more potatoes and cheese than eggs. Which again reminded her of the omelets Kane had made for breakfast.

Impatient with herself, she shook her head. "I think I'll go for the bacon and potato." With green chili.

"You know why they're addictive? They're made with french fries."

"Does the town have a gym? I may need a membership."

MJ laughed. "Girl, you and me, both!"

While the burrito warmed in a toaster oven, Morgan looked over at the sketchpad. "You an artist, in addition to your amazing coffee skills?"

She rolled her eyes back. "I wish. This would be a lot easier if I was."

"What are you working on?"

"So frustrating. I want to run ads on social media, but I can never get my ideas to come across the way I want them to. Never took classes in graphic design, so all my images look as if they were scribbled by a toddler."

"Can I see?"

"Are you an artist?"

"Not even a struggling one! I have neither the inclination nor the aptitude, but I do love wandering the galleries and marveling at other people's talents."

The oven beeped, and Rachel used a huge, industrial spatula to put her food on a white plate.

Even when Rachel slid it in front of her, Morgan didn't move away. "Tell me about your concept."

"I want to feature the custom drinks and capture the vibe."

"Coastal cozy."

"Yes! I love that."

"The pastries here are amazing, and your drinks are divine."

"I brought an idea or two with me from New York." She shrugged. "I had a few shops there."

The information made her realize she knew nothing about Rachel, even though they'd spoken numerous times. Anonymity was one of the things Morgan had been seeking, but now she was learning that she missed connection with other people, especially the Divas with their antics and laughter. "Well, this is better than any place I've ever tried."

"Why thank you." She beamed. "Your food is getting cold."

It was, but she didn't want to walk away. "You might consider hiring a photographer who specializes in food and beverage. There are a bunch of tricks to it."

"I can imagine. My shots come out blurry, and, I don't know, flat-looking. Even I wouldn't be tempted to detour off the highway to try one."

"There are techniques to make even stock photos look wonderful."

"Uh-huh."

Morgan laughed. "Is that skepticism I hear?"

"No, girl. It's full-on disbelief. Anyway, go eat. Please."

After paying and adding a generous tip that more than covered her earlier coffee, she returned to her table.

Instead of scrolling to another video, she browsed stock photography sites, found a few photos she liked, set up accounts to download them, then opened her illustrating program.

An hour later, happier, revved up with creative energy, so focused on what she was doing that time and reality slipped away, she sat back.

In the last sixty minutes, she'd found more purpose than she'd had in weeks. Glad to have been in the zone—something she hadn't realized she'd been missing—she carried her computer to the table where Rachel was wrapping silverware.

"Did you decide on Bali or something for your next stop?"

"Have a look at this." Morgan turned her laptop to show the graphics she'd put together.

"Whoa! What? Are you kidding me right now?" She dropped a fork. "Those are amazing, MJ! Like ah-mazing."

Unaccustomed to that kind of praise, Morgan grinned. "You really like them?" At work, her best efforts had been rewarded with a shrug, a vague "We'll see if that works," and direction to begin writing the accompanying ad copy.

"I love them."

"Give me your email address, and I'll send them to you."

"How much are you going to charge me? I can send you the money right now."

Morgan shook her head. "As you saw, it took no time at all, and I enjoyed doing it."

"Girl, you've been hiding your light. You should let it shine."

Rachel's praise was so good for her. "We can always adjust these basic images for the holidays. Add hearts or a Cupid for Valentine's day. For Christmas, a Santa hat, or a wreath. And we can find some shots of hot chocolate with peppermint sticks. Not saying we should do that, just brainstorming." Which was the part of her job she missed the most.

"I have to pay you for these."

"No. At least not this time."

"Don't you dare do others without letting me compensate you."

"Extra whipping cream and—"

"Double drizzle."

"Is all I need." Together they laughed, and for a moment, Morgan felt like her old self.

Or was that true?

Was she lighter than she recalled being?

"You don't happen to know anything about actual ads, do you? I hear about A/B testing, and I have no idea what it means. Pixies are beyond me."

"I think you mean pixels."

Rachel turned her palms up. "See what I mean?"

"Don't feel bad. It's a skill like everything else. And I can't begin to touch your extraordinary marionberry pie. Which we should definitely photograph."

"I'll get you a piece to take with you."

Rachel cut off her protest with a "Fair's fair, MJ. I can't take without giving."

After being around so many people who didn't share that point of view, Rachel's comments were a breath of fresh air. "Anyway, when you're ready, I'll give you ideas on how to write compelling copy, creating a story. And I'll show you how to split test."

"And pixies?"

With a grin, she met her new-friend's gaze. "And pixies."

"You do this for a living right?"

"Another lifetime ago, I did. But not now."

"You need to set up shop. You could make a boatload of money around here. Everyone needs the help. All of us would like to have a better online presence, but when we're busy, we don't have time. Then when the tourists are gone, we're exhausted."

Until that moment, she hadn't considered it.

Morgan wasn't foolish enough to believe that she'd be an instant success, or a success at all. It was a competitive space. But if she could make enough to cover her living expenses…

Then for the first time, she considered selling her condo, cutting all ties with Colorado.

That felt freeing rather than foolish.

"My email is on here." Rachel offered her business card.

This one, she wouldn't tuck in her pocket and forget. "Expect to hear from me in less than an hour."

"Be careful out there. The rain doesn't seem to want to let up."

Back home, she turned on the heater, powered up her laptop, sent the promised images to Rachel, then started playing with graphics for her new business—not that she was starting one. But it was fun to dream, and it passed the time.

After her caprese salad lunch, her phone rang. *Jennifer.*

"Divas are meeting tonight, and you should be here."

Nachos and margaritas. To go with friendship.

"Since you won't come to us, we're thinking of coming to you."

"What?" She walked to the wdow to look outside while her friend talked.

"It's been forever since we saw you. So Noelle and I are considering a quick getaway. Ella would love to come too, but she and Pierce and the dogs are up at a ranch near Steamboat Springs. They're hiding away from the constant media mess. Both of them were being followed when they went out. It has to die down sometime. Anyway, how's next weekend? Not this one, but the one after. About ten days from now."

"Wait." Morgan shook her head. "Let me catch up."

"You're in Washington, right?"

"No. Oregon."

"All I could remember was that it was somewhere that rains all the time."

Right now, that was certainly true.

"You're in a city, at least, right? Unlike that place in Arizona."

"No."

"You've got an airport nearby though, surely, so you can come pick us up?"

She could only imagine Jennifer's surprise when she looked up the town on a map. "It's called Brook's Bend. Nearest airport is in Eugene, about eighty or ninety miles away."

"Oh." Jennifer exhaled. "We'll rent a car."

"I am on the coast. So there's that. And don't ask about a spa or luxury hotel. There's no such thing here."

"Uhm…" She seemed to search for something positive to say. "Surely you have a good Mexican restaurant?"

After the massive burrito she'd had for breakfast, she could assure her friend that they did, indeed have that.

"Can we stay at your place?"

Jennifer didn't seem at all dissuaded from her decision. "Afraid I only have one bed, but I can recommend a bed-and-breakfast where I stayed."

"So the timing works for you?"

Though it was unexpected, she had no reason to say no. And time with Rachel told her she liked the company. "Check into flights and let me know?"

Jennifer paused for a few seconds. "How are you doing?"

Probably the real reason for the call. "I'm hanging in there."

"Tell me you stopped watching the news every day."

The last time they spoke, that had been her bossy order. "I have."

"And you're getting sunshine and exercise?"

"Yes, ma'am."

"Have you been able to get even one good night's rest?"

She didn't answer.

"Damn it, Morgan. Does this mean you're still thinking about that asshat all the time?"

Kane.

Jennifer let out a great big sigh. "I might kick his butt myself."

She sucked in a sharp breath. Though she shouldn't ask, she had to know… "You've seen him?"

"Morgan…"

"I'm okay. You can tell me."

"He was over the other day. But I'm happy to say he looks

like shit. He deserves it, even though Logan says he was just doing his job. Screw that. This is my friend we're talking about."

They chatted for a few more minutes, with Jennifer giving updates on her upcoming wedding.

Finally, she said she needed to get ready to meet a client. "Anyway, I'll let you know what I find out about the trip. See you soon."

With the call ended and the rest of the day looming in front of her, she put down her phone and wrapped her arms around herself.

How was it possible to be lonelier now than she had ever been?

"Mr. Patterson."

Kane winced. Noelle Montrose stood in the doorway of her mountain home. Unlike the last time he'd been here—what seemed like a lifetime ago—she didn't greet him by his first name, and ice dripped from her tone.

Not that he was surprised.

He'd learned that the Carpe Diem Divas stuck together. Any man who hurt one of them incurred the wrath of them all.

"Joe's in his study. Find your own way."

He nodded as he passed her, but she didn't respond. Once he was inside, she slammed the door closed and rearmed the door. Saying nothing else, she made her way to the kitchen.

Message received, loud and clear. Among their group, he was now a pariah.

Even he agreed he deserved the scorn.

Every damn day, he beat himself up worse than anyone else ever could.

Not long ago, he'd held the most beautiful, kind woman in his arms. She'd turned herself over to him at the club, calling him Sir, allowing him the honor of being her first-ever real Top.

Then when she was in the most dangerous and uncertain time of her entire life, she'd blindly trusted him with her well-being, both physical and emotional.

From their kiss at Joe and Noelle's, he'd known that Morgan had a giving heart and that her feelings lay just beneath the surface—no matter how hard she tried to pretend otherwise.

Fucking asshole that he was, he'd put her personal safety and his sense of duty to the case ahead of her.

Too late, he'd seen that.

From her perspective, he was the world's biggest fuck-up.

From his perspective, she was right.

He'd left her devastated, and she was the last woman on earth who deserved to be treated that way.

He hoped Montrose had some of that damn fine Bonds whiskey available.

After knocking, he entered to find Joe and Logan there, like they had been that fateful night he'd last stepped inside this room.

This time, there was no Hawkeye.

"Heard the front door slam." Joe stood to shake Kane's hand. "The whole damn house shook."

At least it hadn't been in his face. "I'm surprised she let me in."

"So am I." Joe took his seat and poured a couple of fingers of scotch into a glass that he offered to Kane.

Logan lifted his own drink in silent, helpless male sympathy.

"Give the Divas some time," Joe advised.

How many decades?

"Noelle and Jennifer recently returned after having spent some time with Morgan."

Hungry—more desperate than he could imagine—for any scrap of information, he leaned forward.

"They didn't tell me much."

"Where is she?"

"Piss off." Joe took a drink. "Tell you anything, and I risk the wrath of my wife."

He looked to Logan Powell.

"Sorry, buddy. You're on your own."

Man sounded far too damn cheerful.

"Is she doing okay?"

Neither man responded.

Fuck this shit.

After a moment of contemplation, Joe spoke. "You look like something the cat dragged in."

"Should try feeling it from the inside." In his entire life, that might be as close to admitting the truth as he'd ever gotten.

Instead of taking some of his accrued leave, he'd volunteered to be on a couple of personal protection details for one very unpopular Texas senator who was considering a run for president.

Though Kane despised the man and everything he stood for, he did his job and appreciated the fact the constant threats kept him focused for ten or more hours a day.

But at night, in yet another nameless, bland hotel room, he'd grab the phone that never chimed and check the display screen.

After working out and taking a cold shower, he'd scan for news updates about her family, and he'd watch all available videos, hoping to catch a glimpse or mention of Morgan.

Though he could avail himself of Hawkeye resources, he didn't. And not just because it was against the rules—*screw them*—but because she'd gathered the shattered pieces of her emotions and walked away from him.

Realizing he was being morose, he took a sip. "What did I interrupt?"

"Powell was updating me on the case. Our contract with the insurance company has been terminated."

"Can't be related to nonperformance."

Powell shook his head. "Pieces are being recovered, slowly. According to Malloy, the investigator, some are already overseas. Those claims will have to be paid. But their company will be upgrading their security, and Hawkeye landed that contract."

As good as it got.

"And we'll be their firm of record when outside resources are required for investigation."

He tipped his glass toward Powell. "Well done."

"Took all of us. Including you."

Well, the job had been a success, but his personal life was in tatters. Wasn't sure whether that meant a win or a loss.

"It's now an FBI case."

Not a surprise with the mob ties.

"It'll be interesting to watch it play out. See what moves Soren makes. Having a client who confessed—maybe to things she didn't do—has to be interesting."

Montrose nodded. "Wouldn't be surprised if it was his idea. Might have saved her life and those of her loved ones."

If the woman loved anyone—other than her five babies. "Still, she's being represented by a known mob attorney. Clear conflict of interest."

"As long as she's aware and agrees, should be fine," Montrose replied. "Of course I'm no legal scholar."

None of them were. And they'd all spent time skirting the thin line between what was legal and what was necessary. "Any idea how she ended up on a hit list?"

Since it was his case, Powell responded. "Conjecture, but FBI's money is on the bet that she got cold feet—maybe threatened to go to the police. The heists were getting riskier."

As Loughton's death proved.

"We got close to busting them in February."

Not long after Logan had called him for a consult on the case. "When you caught that bullet?"

"Yeah. And it's anyone's guess where Mr. Holden fits in."

From what Kane had seen on the news, the man was standing by his wife. He looked good in a suit, and that played well with audiences and maybe with jurors.

Soren Addison was no fool, a skilled player in media and courtroom theatrics. "She's got a good lawyer." One of the best. As far as Kane knew, none of his clients had served significant time behind bars. Ought to piss off Special Agent Harwood. "If Mrs. Holden refuses to incriminate herself, he might be able to get her off. Create the doubt he needs to. The heat would be off her and the mob."

Powell put down his glass. "I understand a grand jury will be convened."

Which would certainly be a good test of the government's evidence and Soren's case.

An alarm sounded on Joe's phone. "We'll need to wrap this up. Guests will be arriving shortly." He stood.

Kane and Powell followed suit.

"You staying for the play party?" Joe asked.

"No." Only one woman—submissive—interested him.

"Look..." Joe hesitated. "None of my damn business, but you should take some time off. You've been at it straight for how many months? A year?"

More.

"Concur," Powell chimed in.

"Exorcise your demons."

Kane bristled at the observation. "You're saying I have some?"

Apparently not taking offense, Joe bulldozed forward. "No one volunteers to put their life on the line for that bucket of shit senator. Damn right I'm saying something crawled up your ass."

"Your judgment is definitely impaired." Logan added his own assessment.

"Both of you can fuck off."

When Joe continued, it was with less vigor. "Get some rest. Maybe go up to Walker's ranch in Steamboat. From what I hear, we'll be lucky if we get Holden and Ella to ever leave that area."

He followed his coworkers—friends—from the study.

Noelle and Jennifer, Logan's wife, were near the exit, talking loudly.

"Didn't Morgan look great?" Noelle asked.

Though he was on his way out, he stopped. Joe had mentioned they'd seen her.

Jennifer waved a hand in front of her face. "And that hunka-hunka burning love? Only a matter of time before he asks her out."

Kane clamped his back teeth together. The fuck?

Another man?

"I told her it was time to move on." Noelle leaned toward Jennifer. "You know, when a guy you like isn't into you, there's not much you can do."

"Doesn't hurt if the new guy is gorgeous though."

The two giggled.

Then, noticing him, they instantly sobered.

"Jennifer!"

At the sound of her husband's voice, she glanced across the room. Logan crooked his finger, beckoning her and then pointed to the floor in front of him.

"Oh shit." Her shoulders fell. "Me and my big mouth have gotten me into trouble again. My ass is going to be so sore."

"Ugh," Noelle commiserated. "I'm just glad Joe didn't overhear us."

At that moment, Joe cleared his throat, and she swore softly.

"Good night, ladies." The problems that came with being in a relationship.

Fuck if he didn't wish he had them.

Outside in the car, he shot Inamorata a message, asking to be assigned to a task force—anything—as soon as possible.

His phone pinged instantly. Anticipating her customary response of *Acknowledged,* he frowned at her unusual, unexpected response. *Negative.*

The hell?

You're on leave, Patterson. Fourteen days. Have fun.

As if either of them had any clue what the hell that entailed.

Half expecting her to send another message, that she'd been joking and an emergency had arisen, he drove back to Denver.

His phone remained silent, leaving him wondering if either of his well-meaning friends had anything to do with the fact he was now at loose ends and had no idea how in the hell he was going to fill his empty days. And worse…nights.

One thing was sure: if he had the kind of demons that Montrose insisted he did, Kane was never going to be able to outrun them. And that terrified him.

He'd confront a grenade with more confidence than the man whose face was in the mirror.

CHAPTER TEN

HAWKEYE

K ane considered going to the Reserve, but he had no
desire to see Soren or Special Agent Harwood. Now
that he knew who she was and what division she was
assigned to, it was no wonder she spent time at the club
watching Soren. The surprise was that the man let her inside
his business without a warrant.

Potentially a dangerous game of cat and mouse.

Kane shook his head. He'd gotten Inamorata's message
less than five minutes before, and already his mind was refocused on business.

Scoffing, he told himself that was a whole lot better than
regrets or recriminations.

And with that thought, an unwelcome portal opened in
his thoughts, walloping him.

Since he'd had no intention of playing at the party, he
should have refused Joe's invite tonight.

The cold shoulder from Noelle had sliced to the core.

As if that hadn't been enough, his friends hadn't had
much sympathy, and their comments at the end of their

conversation had bordered on brutal. If he were sitting in their seats, he might agree with their assessments.

Guarding the senator while he glad-handed supporters—shaking them down for money at public meetings and fundraisers, refusing to attend town halls where he'd be asked difficult questions—was an assignment for younger, less experienced agents.

God knew Kane had put in his hours of grunt work.

And while doing it, his senses were sharpened, and there was nothing but the job.

As Hawkeye had told him previously, Kane was better suited for strategy. They had plenty of talented men and women who could be assigned to protection but not enough with his particular skillsets, lasering in on patterns and connections, looking at a big picture scenario.

Hawkeye wanted him in an office, maybe working with Inamorata, but he liked field work. Admin gave him hives.

But his hours of work had been for one reason: to forget Morgan and her haunted eyes the moment his betrayal had been laid at her feet.

No matter what he did, he couldn't escape the memory.

He returned home to a cold, soulless space. When Morgan had been here, it had been warmer, brighter. Sharing wine, holding her while she slept, making love to her with the vibrator that was still in his closet... Those were the moments that made life worthwhile.

"Welcome home, Agent Patterson."

Polly's cheery greeting annoyed the crap out of him. "Stuff it."

"Well, hello, Cranky Bastard."

The banter between Polly and Morgan was another thing he missed.

He jogged up the stairs to change into workout clothes,

then told Polly to blast his favorite music through the house. "And turn the lights on full in the exercise room."

"Maybe that will help improve your sparkling personality."

Was everyone a damn critic?

After exhausting himself on the treadmill, pounding out mile after mile, he turned to the punching bag, skipping his hand wraps and gloves. He needed to dissipate his energy in the rawest way possible.

Morgan was interested in someone else?

Or the hunka-hunka burning love was interested in her?

Fuck. Punch.

Fuck. Punch.

Fuck. Punch.

On and on he went, bruising his knuckles, no doubt his hands, creating lacerations. The session should have been more satisfying than it was.

Annoyed, he swiped a towel across his forehead, then threw it into a laundry bin.

After that workout and the number of hours he'd logged at work in recent weeks, exhaustion should plow him under. In case rest was once again elusive, he soaked in the hot tub —blocking out thoughts of one particular brunette beauty— had a shot of whiskey, then took a shower and went to bed— a bed he should be sharing with Morgan.

Three hours later, he was wide awake, and as he shaved, he realized he could no longer outrun his past.

All night, he'd been haunted by images of Morgan, and they'd blended with his former wife, and his failings there.

Noelle and Jennifer's conversation took him back to the past.

He'd been married, and another man had claimed his wife while Kane had been overseas. Maybe if he hadn't been such a cold, unfeeling bastard, that wouldn't have happened.

So what had changed?

He'd become harder. More unfeeling.

In a devastating torrent, Morgan's words came back. *"I've learned my lesson."*

Yeah, he had a job to do, and the decisions he'd made to keep her safe had been good ones.

But his strategy had been fatally flawed.

He hadn't been honest with her about the danger.

Or with himself about his feelings. How could he have been when he'd vowed never again to have any.

But then Morgan had worn her heart on her sleeve, despite the risk he posed, offering something he didn't deserve.

Goddamn it.

With a clatter, his razor dropped onto the counter.

He was in love with Morgan Holden. For better or worse. Richer or poorer. Without her, a piece of his heart was missing.

For sure he was shit at relationships as he'd warned her. But he was shit without her. In that moment, he realized only one thing mattered: having her in his life.

Too bad he didn't deserve her and had no clue what to do.

As she was heading back to her car, Morgan was walking into the wind. Despite the sun's warmth, the air held a bite, and she zipped up her jacket.

Ever since Jennifer and Noelle's visit, Morgan's life had been a whirlwind. Over nachos and margaritas, she'd told the Divas she wasn't coming back—at least not anytime soon.

Even though they were disappointed, they toasted her decision. Not only were they going to arrange to have her condo cleaned out and have her belongings moved into storage, they promised to find a real estate professional to sell her condo.

In return, she agreed to see them every three months. Then she showed them the travel videos she'd bookmarked. Together, they'd planned the next get-together. Since it would be winter, they opted for a resort in San Diego. Before booking the rooms, they called Ella to confirm her schedule.

Once they'd driven away, she'd taken a deep breath and made more decisions. She filed the paperwork for her new business and taught a marketing class at the local library. During a local afterhours meet-up, Rachel introduced her to several local business owners who seemed interested in her services. But Rachel hadn't stopped there. She'd raved about Morgan's talents to friends in New York.

In addition to securing her first paying clients, she was also freelancing for a major ad agency on the East Coast.

She'd found a small house that she was interested in renting, and she planned to sign the lease later in the afternoon.

All of this should have made her ecstatic. But her heart was still shattered.

When she least expected it, overwhelming loneliness crashed into her, leaving her vulnerable.

No matter how many times she told herself that she should have protected herself better, she now realized she couldn't have.

Kane had unapologetically told her he was who he was.

The time had come to face the fact that she was who she was.

No matter how hard she struggled to suppress her emotions, they were still there, bubbling just beneath the surface.

And she decided that was okay.

Rachel had suggested that tapping into her emotion could be an asset in her work. Even Morgan had to admit that the graphics she'd recently created had been some of her best ever. The marketing director in New York had called several of them evocative.

Was it because she was no longer dealing with the stress of being employed at her father's company? Or because she was no longer trying to be someone she wasn't?

Either way, she looked forward to arriving at Seaside Sips every morning and pulling out her laptop.

Twenty minutes later, she pulled into her usual parking spot, grabbed her computer, and headed inside.

"Hey, MJ! The usual?"

"Extra whipping cream."

And then a man's voice washed over her. "Double drizzle."

Her knees weakened, and her lips parted.

Slowly, ever so slowly, she turned to see Kane sitting at a nearby table. As she met his gaze, he stood. "What…?" This couldn't be happening. There was no way he was in her favorite coffee shop that was a million miles from anywhere.

"Buy you a coffee?"

"Kane." Her heart raced as every part of her being responded to him, the untamed husk of vulnerability in his tone, the tiny lines grooved next to his dark eyes, and the way his hair was shoved back from his forehead, as if he'd repeatedly dragged his hands through it.

"I'd like to talk to you."

She tried to put on a brave front. "There's nothing more to be said."

"Five minutes?"

"How did you find me?" *And why were you looking?*

His half smile was wry and exhausted. "That explanation will take considerably longer than five minutes."

How could he be more handsome than she remembered, so devastating? "Hawkeye?"

"No. I'd be fired for that, or Hawkeye would have sent me back to Africa so fast I wouldn't know what hit me."

Even now, the idea of him being in such a risky place, his life on the line, terrified her. It shouldn't matter, but it did.

"Patterns. Connections."

She scowled. Even she hadn't known where she'd end up.

Rachel joined them. Studying Morgan intently, she extended the coffee cup toward her. "Everything okay?"

Was it? And how did she explain what he'd meant to her? "We're old…" *Lovers. Dominant and sub.* She settled for something that was the absolute, flat truth. "I'm a former client of his."

At the description, he winced. "Kane Patterson," he introduced himself. "You make an excellent cup of coffee."

Rachel ignored his outstretched hand. "Holler if you need me, MJ."

"Thank you."

"She's tough."

"We look out for each other."

"Good."

Still standing, not wanting to join him at a table as that seemed to invite familiarity, she took her first sip. "Finish your explanation."

"That night in the hot tub. You talked about the night sky. The stars. Which made me think you might not choose a big city."

Impressive. "Go on."

"You've always called Denver and the mountains your home." When she didn't respond, he continued. "So I narrowed it down to states with mountains."

"There are plenty of them."

"And a lot of times when people want to get away, they drive until they run out of road. I figured once you left your condo, you'd head west. You can be in the Rockies, anonymous, in under an hour."

"Still the West Coast has a lot of coastline."

"You filed incorporation papers."

The blood drained from her face.

"A coffee shop is a logical place to look, and I gambled that you wouldn't change your habits. There are a few others around. But the social media pages for this one are a cut above. And since you've started a marketing business... A guess, maybe. But it fits the connections I talk about."

"That's a lot of effort."

"You're worth it."

"Please..." She closed her eyes. *Don't hurt me again.* If she was smart, she'd tell him his time was up and walk away. But damn her soft heart. She couldn't do that.

"Tell me I've earned five minutes."

"Yes. But not here."

"Anywhere you say."

"There's a park bench overlooking the ocean that I like. I need to pay for my coffee before I go."

"Told you I'd buy you one." He crossed to the counter and placed a twenty-dollar bill on it.

"Doesn't impress me, Mr. Kane Patterson," Rachel said.

"Good. I like that MJ has people looking out for her."

"I wrote down your license plate number. And your name."

Two protectors, facing off.

When he returned to her, Morgan said, "We'll take separate cars so I can leave when your time is up."

For a moment, he appeared to consider an argument. Then he nodded tightly.

As she drove over to the small parking lot near her favorite bench, he kept his rental car close to her bumper, tailgating as if she might try to make a getaway. Not that it would do her any good.

Then, when they were seated on opposite ends of the bench, she took a sip of her coffee to calm her nerves, then checked her watch. "Time's ticking."

He reached into his pocket to pull out a piece of paper.

"What's that?"

"My notes."

"Notes?" He'd written this down? His efforts touched her.

"I didn't know if you'd give me five minutes, and I wanted to be sure I didn't forget anything. So it's in order. And now I've wasted thirty seconds." He cleared his throat.

Was... Was he nervous?

Big, strong secret agent man couldn't find this situation unnerving.

Unflinchingly, he met her gaze. "Even if I get only one thing out, I want it to be this. I'm sorry."

"For?"

"Hurting you."

That didn't even begin to cover it.

He slid his finger to the second item on his list. "I don't deserve you. I never did."

Struggling to hold back the tears that suddenly stung her eyes, she blinked rapidly.

"Those are the two important things, but I also owe you an explanation. If you want it."

Maybe that would give her closure, help her to forget him.

"I've always kept my emotions locked away. I was loyal to my wife, but that wasn't enough. Not nearly enough. So when I lost that marriage, and the baby I thought for a moment that I might be having, I doubled down on my losing strategy. The truth was, when I kissed you at Joe and Noelle's wedding, I wanted you so bad it hurt. And I knew what I did to my ex. So I shut you down. Shut myself down. I didn't want to be a bastard again. And irony, right? I became an even worse one."

"Anything else on your list?"

"One remaining item." He carefully folded the piece of paper, and as he did so, she noticed how sharp the edges were, as if he'd repeatedly opened it and studied the contents.

He took a breath, slipped it back into his pocket, then looked at her with emotion she'd never before seen in his eyes. "I love you."

Her coffee slipped from her hand.

It crashed into the rocky ground beneath them, the lid skittering away.

They both ignored it.

"You...?"

"With my heart and my soul."

He'd used up his five minutes, and she was too stunned to stop him from going on.

"I've made a lot of mistakes. Out of all of them, the worst was not telling you what I was feeling. At the end, you were left guessing. And here's a brutal truth that I've had to face. I'm a coward."

Frantically she shook her head.

"I couldn't tell you what you meant to me because I couldn't admit it to myself. All along you've been honest and upfront while I focused on doing my job, as if that was the only thing that mattered." He turned one palm up. "When in truth, your wellbeing—mental, emotional, physical—were all equally as important. In that I failed you."

He raked his hand into his hair. "You've given me more than you ever need to, including now. You've allowed me to go over my time allotment." Then, with a sigh, he stood and turned to walk away.

From her life. Forever.

"I..." Morgan didn't know what to say, to think. But her heart was ready to explode. Once again, was she facing her own heartbreak? "Kane..."

He stopped and slowly pivoted.

"Stay." Would she regret this? Maybe. But she'd regret it more if she let him go. He'd worked hard to find her, ridiculously so, skipping the resources he could have used, because she mattered. "Why did you come looking for me? And I don't mean the nice words on your paper."

"Because I love you and want to spend my life with you."

"You mean it?"

"Every word. I want to spend my days—and my nights—deserving you, earning your love. I'm not perfect—"

Despite the solemnity, she couldn't help but smile. "Even Polly knows that."

"Even she's sick of me, and as far as I know, she's programmed to put up with all human bullshit."

"Cranky bastard."

"More so than normal."

Then suddenly, he looked at her, and his eyes filled with longing. In this moment, he was everything. Protector. Bodyguard. Secret agent. Military operative. "I've fucked up. But damn it, at least for this moment, I'm following the path that you blazed by being honest. I want to marry you. All the vows, every promise, always and forever."

"I love you." Her confession was shrouded in her tears. "But I don't know how this would work." Was she close to having everything she wanted, only to have it yanked away?

She stood to pick up the coffee cup and find the lid. As she made her way to the trash can, she allowed herself to get lost in the never-ending ocean view.

Thoughts in turmoil, she sat back down next to him. "I love it here. With everything that happened in Denver, I'm...

I've started a new life. Making friends, becoming part of the community. I'm signing a lease this afternoon."

"Understood. You're saying no. There's no place in your life for me as your husband."

"That's not what I'm implying." For a man so good at puzzles, how had he gotten that so wrong?

Before going on, he gulped. "You love me?"

"Yes."

He pressed his palms together. "So we can start from there? Do you want to be with me?"

"Did you hear me a minute ago?"

"Morgan, do you want to be with me?"

More than anything in the world. "Yes. These are the words I've dreamed of hearing from you." But never believed he'd say them.

"I understand that you don't want to come back to Denver. I've been all around the world and never called anywhere else home. But wherever you are is where my new home will be. If it's the godforsaken Oregon coast, then that's what it is."

"What about your job? Your need for work? Action? Danger?"

"I'm ready to turn that in for a different kind of challenge. Logistics. Big picture stuff. Potentially remote work."

"You're willing to give all that up?"

"Not the way I see it." That emotion made his voice crack again. "I'd be giving up nothing and gaining everything."

"Kane... I don't know what to say." It was a dream come true.

"Two words is all I'm looking for."

He lowered himself to one knee and once again reached inside his jacket. This time, he brought out a small box.

Her heart stopped.

"Morgan, will you marry me?"

In that moment, he made her heart whole again. Tears of joy and happiness slid from her eyes as she laughed and smiled at the same time. "Oh, Kane! I love you. Yes, yes, yes, yes. Yes, I'll marry you."

He slid the stunning diamond onto her finger, and the fit was perfect.

"How did you know the right size?"

"I know everything about you, every single detail." He stood and swept her into his arms, off her feet to spin her around.

When he finally set her down, she was dizzy, her world exploding with joy.

He kissed her deeply until the response threatened to overtake them both. "Do you have a place I can take you? Or shall I get us a hotel?"

"There's not much that's fancy around here."

"As long as we have a bed and can get started on our future…"

"Uhm, Kane…" She looked up at him through wide eyes, not daring to hope. "Are you saying what I think you are?"

"That I'd love to have children with you? Get you pregnant and spoil you rotten?"

She blinked. He'd turned her life upside down. Again. "But what about—"

"Spanking your ass and tying you up." He lowered his voice to that timber that rocketed shivers through her. "Make you call me Sir? All that, Morgan. Everything. I've told you I am who I am. That's no longer true. I will strive to be the man you deserve. Nothing held back. Now and forever."

"In that case, let's get started with the future."

Five weeks later, after a celebratory dinner at the Mexican restaurant where she'd had dinner with the Divas, Kane carried her across the threshold of their new house. Rather than renting, Kane had opted to buy them a place with two offices since they were both working from home.

Not surprising her, Hawkeye had asked him to join forces with Inamorata in planning and strategy, and so far the position seemed to suit him. He'd have to fly back on occasion, and Morgan was always free to remain or travel with him. She'd gone with him once so far, to see her friends. But other than missing them and Pierce, and even the dogs who were perfectly happy with Pierce and Ella, Morgan couldn't be happier with her life.

He'd equipped the house with a state-of-the-art alarm and an upgraded version of Polly that was equally as sassy as the one in Denver. She enjoyed having a chief of staff. Much more than Kane did.

Their three bedrooms gave them room for their family to grow or to have company, including the Divas. To her, the relationship had moved at warp speed. He'd disagreed. They'd lost out on the last two years, time they would have had if he'd taken her to bed the night they'd met.

They could sell later, if their lives changed. Or keep it as a romantic getaway.

They'd spent a lot of time talking, and he'd told her about Noelle and Jennifer giving their relationship a little nudge. Not that he'd needed it. Once he stopped trying to outrun his thoughts, the truth was staring at him. He couldn't live without her.

She was secretly grateful to her friends. They'd known how miserable she was, and they'd known she would never take the first step toward reconciliation.

"I'm thinking we should try out the bed, Mrs. Patterson."

Even though they weren't married, he wanted her to get

accustomed to the sound of her new name. Frankly she liked it. "I agree."

He carried her to their suite and placed her on the bed before pulling off her shoes and sliding a hand beneath her skirt.

"Ah. No panties."

Her gaze turned hazy. "No, Sir."

"Good girl." It was a growl, a promise, as he sat on the edge of the mattress. "Now undress for me."

Exaggerating her movements, taking her time, she did so. Then when he shot her a purposeful glance, she lowered herself into position.

"I love you, Golden Eyes."

"Show me how much, Sir."

Purposefully, rhythmically, he did.

When he was done, and she'd whimpered through half a dozen orgasms he gathered her close. "Welcome home, sweetheart."

She snuggled into him. "There's no place I'd rather be than in your arms."

◊ ◊ ◊ ◊ ◊

I appreciate you reading Determination. I hope you love Kane as much as I do. This protector hero was more complex than I imagined when I first started writing him, and I had no idea how falling for Morgan would change his heart and soul so completely.

If you're intrigued about the Reserve world, and Master Soren—is he a good guy or not?—book one in that series is available now.

And if you love bodyguards and protectors, there are plenty of other deliciously Dominant heroes in the Hawkeye series. Each book stands alone, so you can find the type of story you love most.

I'd like to introduce you to the ultra-sexy cowboy and former military operative Jacob Walker... Jacob can't refuse one last mission, protecting the beautiful, fiery Elissa. But she refuses to be whisked away from her life like a terrified damsel in distress. But that's exactly what happens when she's thrown over the muscular shoulder of one very inflexible, annoying, and handsome, alpha bodyguard.

Once she's at his remote ranch near Steamboat Springs, Colorado, she discovers something much more dangerous than the threat facing her—her very real attraction to the smoking-hot captor who will not let her go.

DISCOVER HOLD ON TO ME

Don't miss out! VIP newsletter subscribers receive special bonus reads—epilogues, deleted scenes, and more. Of course, you'll get all the insider news about upcoming releases, special promotions, and sales. Become a VIP newsletter subscriber today!

VIP Reader newsletter

Do you love ultra-sexy and ridiculously rich Dominants? Please join me at The Reserve where former military operative and Dominant Nathaniel Stratton will stop at nothing to claim her—heart, body, trust, and soul—forever.

Covert operator and former military officer Nathaniel Stratton is focused on protecting his country. He has no time for relationships or love.

While on leave back home, helping to run the very secret, very sexy BDSM club he co-owns, he's captivated by one of his employees, the beautifully obedient Alani Dane.

For years, Alani has been hiding a secret. She trusts no

one, especially not the sexy, relentless billionaire determined to taste her surrender. But with every kiss and touch, he tears down a little more of the fortress she's built around her heart.

When danger spirals out of control and her worst nightmare is realized, Alani has no choice but to count on masterful alpha Nathaniel. Will the cost of his protection be too high a price to pay?

★★★★★ "Packed with all the delicious feels you need." ~Amazon Reviewer

★★★★★ "Full of exciting adventure, mystery, suspense, and steamy situations that are so riveting that I couldn't put it down until the very last page." ~Amazon Reviewer

DISCOVER TEASE ME

Turn the page for an exciting excerpt from TEASE ME:

TEASE ME EXCERPT

A loud knock on Alani's boss's office door pierced the silence.

"Come in!" her boss called.

Wondering who dared interrupt the meeting where she was being reprimanded for yawning during a submissive scene with a customer, Alani gave into the temptation to turn around.

Master Nathaniel.

He left her breathless, but at this moment, she'd rather deal with the devil.

The ridiculously handsome and rigid man regarded her before closing the door. His mouth was set in a firm, uncompromising line. But his green eyes sent a shiver of frost down her spine.

"I invited Master Nathaniel to join us since he'll be running the club for a few days while I'm away."

Stunned, she broke her gaze away from Master Nathaniel's to stare, agog at Master Soren. "You're leaving, Sir?" The evening had gone from bad to disastrous.

"Family business." As vague as ever, he waved a hand.

Moments later Master Nathaniel dragged back the chair next to her and took a seat. He was so large his knee brushed hers. Electrified—and horrified by her reaction—she scooted away.

He cleared his throat to hide his quick smile. Damnable Dom.

"Bring me up to speed, Alani."

She frowned. "In what way? You know what happened during my scene with Sir Richard. You were there."

He steepled his hands. "Explain it in your words."

In one sentence, he'd gone from nemesis to asshole.

"I've already gone over it with Master Soren."

"And I'm in charge now, and I asked you a direct question."

Intensity radiated from him, unnerving her. "I assured Master Soren it won't happen again. That's all you need to know."

His eyebrows furrowed, a storm cloud gathering. "You may not want to add insubordination to the list of your sins, little sub."

And maybe she did.

He glanced at Soren. "I'd like a few minutes alone with Alani if you don't mind."

She gulped.

Master Soren dropped his pen to the desktop as he nodded.

What the hell? Alani cleared her throat. "Wait a minute."

"Alani?" Master Soren asked.

For a brief second, she was tempted to use the club's safe word, but she didn't want to give either of them the satisfaction of knowing how badly Master Nathaniel rattled her. "That's fine. I can deal with Master Nathaniel." She buried her niggle of doubt beneath a pile of bravado.

The door clicked shut behind Master Soren, leaving her

alone with the terrifying Dominant. The atmosphere crackled, chasing up her spine like lightning.

He tilted his head, and she remembered the powerful way he'd captured her chin and forced her attention back to the scene.

Instinct urged her to run, hard, far, and fast. Her traitorous body refused to obey her brain's command. Part of her looked forward to the upcoming challenge with a ferocity that bordered on desperation. In this moment, even though it was unwanted, excitement pinged through her. She was more alive than she'd been in months.

He leaned slightly toward her.

Refusing to shrink away, she straightened her spine.

"When I ask a question, Alani, I expect an honest and quick answer." Tight, leashed energy vibrated in his tone.

In spite of her resistance, every part of her responded to his power.

"Am I clear?"

"You are."

He nodded. The slight acknowledgment that she pleased him scattered tiny pulses of pleasure through her.

"Talk to me. I'm listening." He spoke with intensity but in a softer, more compelling tone. The man knew how to use his voice in a way that made her thoughts fracture. "Give me an explanation for your behavior."

He regarded her. His fierce green eyes were cold, and she wondered what they would look like if they weren't? If he desired her? If he were her Dom? She squirmed. Where the hell had that thought come from?

"Alani?"

"It wasn't so much that I allowed my mind to wander."

He waited, and she realized he would never be satisfied with the answers she'd given Master Soren.

Master Nathaniel wanted the unvarnished truth. But if

she gave it, if she admitted how out of control her personal life was, she might lose her job.

"It's not enough for you, is it?"

"What?" She opened her mouth, then closed it without speaking. He was more perceptive than she'd given him credit for. Then, choosing her words with great care, she responded to his question. "I'm not sure what you're talking about."

"You are."

Despite all her inner resolve, she scooted to the far side of her chair. He saw too much of her, and he was determined to excavate her deepest secrets—secrets she was determined to keep.

With infinite patience, he remained silent, allowing time to drag.

"Master Soren said I needed to go home for the evening. If you'll excuse me...?" She stood.

"Certainly your call. But we'll have this same conversation again tomorrow. What time do you report? Four o'clock? I'll have Harmony calendar our meeting."

Uncompromising bastard.

She moved to the window, putting distance between them. How much to reveal, without telling the whole truth? "There's no excuse for what happened tonight. I'm tired. As I told Master Soren, I didn't sleep well, and I'll endeavor to do better."

"And the reason for that?"

"It happens to everyone at some point."

"Does it?"

Maybe not to the superhuman alpha.

In that damnable, patient way, he waited as if he had nothing better to do.

With a sigh, she relented. "You're right. There's part of me that craves something more."

"I'd like to hear more. Go on, please."

Confused by his soft, inviting tone, she frowned. This side of him was potent, and maybe even more threatening to her equilibrium. "Ever since I discovered BDSM, I've used it as a stress relief."

"And stress keeps you awake?"

Unable to deny the truth, she nodded.

"A vicious cycle."

"I'll step up my workouts." In fact she already had, but so far it hadn't helped.

"You're not getting what you need from scening with club Tops?"

She nodded.

"And you have no one you play with?"

They were getting into deep, personal waters where it might be impossible for her to hide. Protecting herself, Alani brought her chin up. "This isn't an appropriate work discussion."

"We can stop at any time. You're not required to answer." He lifted one shoulder. "I'm merely interested."

On some level, she wanted this—a relentless man to see her struggles, help her cut through them, refuse to accept a half-hearted answer. "No. I have no one."

"You're taking care of others, but you have no outlet for your own stress?"

If he had any idea how close those words hit…

She shook her head to clear the troubling emotions rattling through her brain. He was right. But how did she confess that to him? Not only was he her boss, he was a near stranger.

"When was the last time you got what you needed?"

"I don't know." She frowned. "Months. Maybe a year." Becoming a submissive had seemed like a perfect job. Now she was realizing it had taken her further away from the release she hungered for.

"Is that what you want? Something real? Something that will leave a mark? Something to take you away?"

God. Yes. She met his steely gaze.

"It's been a while for me too."

Her blood turned sluggish before surging. "Is that an invitation?" If so, how could she dare say yes?

This was out of bounds in all the ways...

While he wasn't technically her boss, he was for the immediate future. And he was an owner in the company.

"Of course we'd need to have rules in place."

He was offering her a gift. But was accepting too high a price to pay?

"We couldn't do it here."

She nodded, but it wasn't in agreement. If they were to scene, they would need to go somewhere else.

"You'd have to ask for it. Beg, even. I'd want you in front of me on your knees."

She sucked in a breath as she scanned his features, looking for giveaways in his expression. "Are you teasing me?"

"Absolutely not." Nathaniel shook his head. "There'd be no pretense. No acting like you do with other men. I want your unadulterated, raw need."

From the relative safety of the other side of the room, she studied him, noting the strength of his forearms, the honed angles of his body. He was a warrior, accustomed to battle. His strength and mental acuity awed her.

Every instinct warned that submitting to him would be unlike anything she'd ever experienced.

"How brave are you?"

ABOUT THE AUTHOR

I invite you to be the very first to know all the news by subscribing to my very special **VIP Reader newsletter**! You'll find exclusive excerpts, bonus reads, and insider information.

https://www.sierracartwright.com/subscribe/

For tons of fun and to join with other awesome people like you, join my Facebook reader group: **Sierra's Super Stars**

https://www.facebook.com/groups/SierrasSuperStars

And for a current booklist, please visit my **website**:

http://www.sierracartwright.com

USA Today bestselling author Sierra Cartwright was born in England, and she spent her early childhood traipsing through castles and dreaming of happily-ever afters. She has two wonderful kids and four amazing grand-kitties. She now calls Galveston, Texas home and loves to connect with her readers. Please do drop her a note.

ALSO BY SIERRA CARTWRIGHT

<u>Titans</u>

Sexiest Billionaire

Billionaire's Matchmaker

Billionaire's Christmas

Determined Billionaire

Scandalous Billionaire

Ruthless Billionaire

<u>Titans Quarter</u>

His to Claim

His to Love

His to Cherish

<u>Titans Quarter Holidays</u>

His Christmas Gift

His Christmas Wish

His Christmas Wife

<u>Titans Sin City</u>

Hard Hand

Slow Burn

All-In

<u>Titans Captivated (Ménages)</u>

Theirs to Hold

Theirs to Love

Theirs to Wed

Theirs to Treasure

Titans: Reserve

Tease Me

Hawkeye

Come to Me

Trust in Me

Meant For Me

Hold On To Me

Believe in Me

Hawkeye: Denver

Initiation

Determination

Temptation

Bonds

Crave

Claim

Command

Donovan Dynasty

Bind

Brand

Boss

Mastered

With This Collar

On His Terms

Over The Line

In His Cuffs

For The Sub

In The Den

Collections

Titans Series

Titans Billionaires: Firsts

Titans Billionaires: Volume 1

Billionaires' Quarter: Titans Quarter Collection

Risking It All: Titans Sin City Collection

Yours to Love: Titans Captivated Collection

Hawkeye Series

Here for Me: Volume One

Beg For Me: Volume Two

Printed in Great Britain
by Amazon

20307588R00129